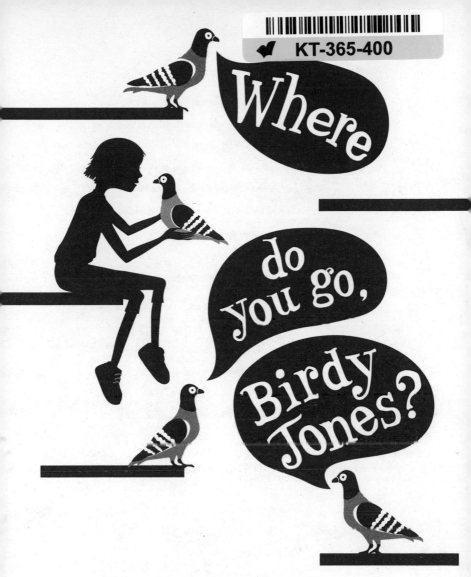

Where do you go, Birdy Jones?

JOANNA NADIN

LITTLE, BROWN BOOKS FOR YOUNG READERS

LITTLE, BROWN BOOKS FOR YOUNG READERS

First published in Great Britain in 2018 by Hodder and Stoughton

1 3 5 7 9 10 8 6 4 2

A CIP catalogue record for this book
is available from the British Library.

ISBN 978-1-51020-126-2

Printed and bound by CPI Group (UK) Ltd, Croydon, CR0 4YY

The paper and board used in this book are made
from wood from responsible sources.

Little, Brown Books for Young Readers
An imprint of
Hachette Children's Group
Part of Hodder and Stoughton
Carmelite House
50 Victoria Embankment
London EC4Y 0DZ

An Hachette UK Company
www.hachette.co.uk

www.hachettechildrens.co.uk

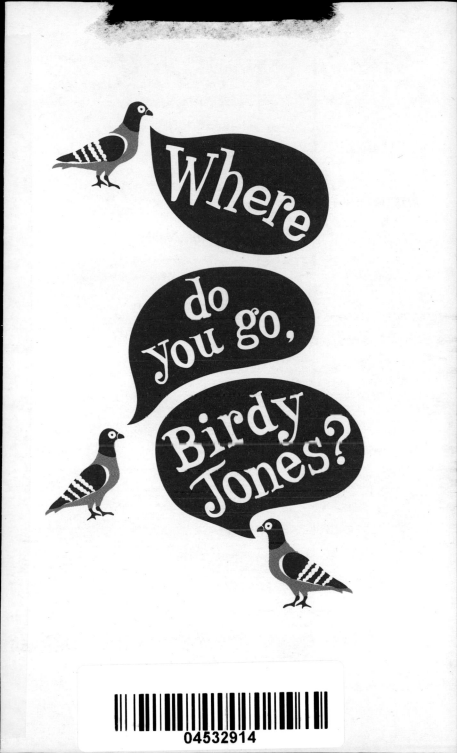

Also by Joanna Nadin

Joe All Alone

White Lies, Black Dare

The Incredible Billy Wild

For Michael, who loves Leeds

Dogger

Birdy don't rightly know who he is or where he come from. Maybe from up the estate beyond the main road, maybe from just round the corner, he don't like to say. He just shows up, appears from the thick dusty air in the pigeon loft, or out of the trees up Cop Hill. Not a ghost or a phantasm, just a boy her age or thereabouts.

But there's a magic to him. To his hair, spun like Rapunzel's, with strands of red and gold; to his clothes, half charity shop, half dressing-up box; to his name, not a boy's but not quite animal either. Dogger. Plain but odd.

Like her, she supposes.

The first time Dogger comes, Birdy's six and sobbing in the loft. It's because of Sadie – Sadie from the back of Dad's cab, Sadie with her too-big hair and her too-bright clothes and her chit-chat, chit-chat all about the telly. Birdy don't know what Dad sees in her. Sadie's no different to all the other women he went out with before her – Fat Sue, Carol from the bookies, Mad Maxine. None of them lasted more than a few months, with their preening and then their pecking when Dad – and Birdy – didn't measure up. Only somehow Sadie's stuck, taking up time Dad should've spent with Birdy, and taking up space in the house, moving into their nest like a no-good cuckoo, filling it with her frilly curtains and fancy pillows and making herself a feather bed to lie in.

But that's not the worst of it.

No, now she's having a baby.

When Birdy thinks about that, about having to share her dad not just with Sadie but with the gaping gob of a mewling little'un and all, she lets out another terrible squawk. And Dogger must have heard the noise – her *haw-haw* that's turned the birds' soft hum and trill into ruffled feathers and restless pacing – and come to see who she is, and why she's being a cry-baby.

"Hello," he says.

Birdy looks up chip-chop, wipes snot on her arm. Then her mouth gapes and words stopper in her gob as she sees him in the doorway, a halo of July sun on hair spun from copper and a set of – blimey! – wings. "Who are you?" she asks. "Are – are you a bird? Or . . . or an angel?" Sadie believes in angels, reckons she's got one watching her from heaven. Sadie . . . Another fat sob racks through Birdy and she clacks her teeth together to clamp it in.

He steps towards her, hands on hips, bare feet

on splintered boards. "I'm not an angel, and I'm definitely not a flaming bird," he says. Then he cracks his face open with a smile as wide as the Pennines. "I'm Dogger."

In the dim fust of the loft she can make out her mistake. He's dressed in a tight green catsuit that clings like skin, stapled all over with crepe paper leaves, and on his back a pair of feathered fancy-dress wings. The kind Sadie got for a fiver from Costcutter and made her wear for Halloween. The kind Birdy snatched off and stamped into the mud of the back garden first chance she got. Flaming fairies, she'd said to herself. Flaming fairies ... until Dad had picked them up, and her, and made her wash them, and her mouth out and all.

Birdy smiles back at the boy and says, "Dogger's a funny name."

"S'pose," he replies, peering into the perches, stretching out thin fingers to stroke a bird. "What's yours?"

She hesitates, not knowing which one to tell

4

him. In the end she picks both. "Birdy," she replies. "It were Bridie, once upon a time, but my dad says no one called me that, not ever, not even before I worked with the birds. Now only Miss Higgins calls me Bridie."

"Birdy's not so normal," says Dogger.

"I know that," she snaps, playground chants echoing in her ears. She rubs them to shut out the noise. "What are you meant to be, anyway?"

He looks down at his greenness. "The god of something," he replies. "Only my mam's not so good with sewing."

"Oh, I don't know," says Birdy. 'Cause Sadie's never sewn more than a button back on for her.

Dogger sits down in Grandpa's green chair, picks a crusty scab of pigeon poo off the arm. "So, why're you crying," he asks.

"I'm not," she insists.

"You were," he says. "I saw you."

Birdy bristles. "Sadie's having a baby," she says. "A girl. 'Least it will be. It's just a peanut now, so she reckons. And they're getting married and all. So there's no getting rid now. Not ever."

Dogger nods. "Sadie your mam?"

"No!" Birdy shakes her head, indignant. "She's not my mam, she's a mobile hairdresser. But my dad – my dad ..."

"Yer dad thinks the sun shines out of her backside, I bet."

"Aye. Only it don't and I told her that and all and then I come here."

"What about your real mam?" Dogger asks. "The one that had you?"

Birdy shrugs like she don't know. And truth be told, she don't, not much. But the bits she does she hands him like they're jewels. "She died when I were three. She had red hair and green eyes. And she loved books more than anything."

"So Sadie's your wicked stepmother?"

Birdy thinks about this. About the storybook women who send their children out into the woods with nowt but breadcrumbs. Or give them poisoned apples to eat. "She give me a hamster once," she tells him by way of an answer. "Dave, it were called. Only she told me I couldn't call a hamster Dave."

"Why not?" he asks.

"That's what I said," says Birdy. "Only Sadie tells me it's got no dignity. Bad as calling a bird Billy."

"Billy's a good name for a bird."

"Aye," says Birdy. "A bobby dazzler, Grandpa reckons. It run off in the end when I were cleaning it out."

"Who, Dave?"

Birdy feels her lips twitch and turn up at the corners, feels something inside her stretch its wings out and lift. "No, me dad," she jokes.

Dogger grins, wide as a pelican, warming Birdy as if he's the sun himself.

"Anyway, Sadie said I weren't allowed pets after that."

"You got birds, though."

"Aye," says Birdy, smiling herself now. "She'll not take them away. Not 'til hell freezes, Grandpa says."

Dogger nods, like he knows the truth of it.

"You got a sister?" she asks him then.

"No way," Dogger says. "Nor a brother and don't want one, neither. Too much noise. And poo."

Birdy laughs and snot flies out of her nose on to her sundress. She wipes it in, not bothered at the smear.

"Anyway," Dogger carries on. "My dad's too busy for babies. He's an international jewel thief."

"No, he in't. Is he?" Birdy's eyes widen as she imagines a man dangling in a suit and snatching a diamond from a black-velvet display case.

"I reckon." Dogger shrugs. "What about yours?"

Birdy sighs. "He were a swimmer once," she says. "But that didn't work out, so then he were a postman, like my Grandpa Jones were. Only he couldn't read the letters proper so Big Al – he was the boss – he had to let Dad go and now he drives a cab. It's a Ford Mondeo," she adds. "With under-seat heating."

"Nice." Dogger nods, and Birdy blooms, but briefly.

"Only Julie Gilhoolie was sick in it last Friday and it smells, though he'd still rather drive the cab than spend time with me."

Dogger says something. Something he shouldn't and Birdy sucks in air, sharp. "That's a swear," she hisses.

"So?" says Dogger. "Who's to hear it? Just me and you."

Birdy listens. Grandpa's still inside the house, asleep, she reckons, or watching Leeds United on the telly. So she says the swear herself, only soft, whispering. She's not that brave. Not really. Not yet.

Dogger smiles. "I know what'll cheer you up." He scrambles up so he's stood on the chair, feet sinking into springs and threadbare nylon.

"What?" Birdy asks, pushing herself to her feet, caught in the excitement.

"A song."

"A song?" Birdy feels disappointment slosh over her like school custard. What's so good about a song?

"It's a special one, honest." Dogger puts his hands on his hips again. "Listen," he says, and begins.

Birdy listens, to the up-down, up-down of the notes, to the words about birds — three of them, little ones — fat words that burst with love and sunshine and the tight arms of a hug; words that tug-tug-tug at a thread inside her, pull out a memory, ripe as a plum. "I know this song," she realises. "I know it!" And she sings along, soft at first, like the swear, then louder, not caring who hears it, not caring when Grandpa comes trip-trapping up the rickety plank to see what all the fuss is about; not caring when Mrs Housden from number four says, "Blimey, Birdy," as she dances round the corner on her way back home; not caring when Sadie glowers at her through the window, still nursing her hurt like she's nursing that peanut thing inside her.

Dad cuts her off, though, soon as she walks in the door. "Where've you been?" he asks. "You don't just stomp off like that."

"Up at the pigeon loft," she says. "I learned a song." And she sings him a line.

"Who taught you that?" he says, his face pale as the thin milk Sadie pours on her cereal.

"Dogger," she says. "He turned up at the loft, just walked in. Reckon he must live round there. He says—"

But Dad don't want to hear what Dogger's got to say and he cuts her off quick. "That's enough. I don't want you hanging round with . . . with odd boys. Where was your grandpa?"

"In the house," Birdy says. "Leeds won," she adds.

"Aye, well." Dad ponders. "Just . . . just . . . no

storming off again. And no Dogger and no . . . no singing about little birds, all right?"

"What's wrong with the song?" Birdy asks.

"Nowt. I just . . . I never liked it. That's all."

Birdy nods a promise, then runs upstairs to wash her hands, but it's already too late. Dogger's song has caught in her hair, and stuck to the soles of her feet. It slip-slides into her thoughts when she's supposed to be eating, sleeping, subtracting sixty-seven from two hundred and five and timesing it all by eleven. "Three little birds," she sings in her head, as she stamps out of the school gates the next day. "Three little birds," she sings, as she pulls off her sandals and puts on her wellies. "Three little birds," she sings, as she sits on the steps of the pigeon loft and waits for the boy with the wings to fly back and make every little thing all right.

And he does.

When her sister, Minnie, were born early and she were too small, and no one knew if she would make it through each night, Dogger listened when Birdy were sorry she'd wished all the bad on her, sorry she wished she weren't having a sister.

When Sadie and her dad got wed, and she had to wear that flaming dress and hold her sister's hand and smile-smile-smile like it were the bees knees when all she wanted to do was sob. That time Dogger told her jokes until she were smiling for real and the wedding were nowt but a day ticked off on the kitchen calendar.

When her dad crashed the taxi, and all the money they had for a month was Sadie's and all they had for tea was beans. That time Dogger told her that sometimes, when his mam were ill, all they had for tea was stories, and that words filled his stomach better than bread ever could.

When her pigeon Marilyn got tossed from Cop Hill for the first time and they waited, waited, fists clenched, breath baited, for her to come home. Then Dogger stood by her side, clenched his fists too, and squeezed her hand when the bird plopped on to her perch like she'd only been out for a five-minute flap.

Birdy's eleven now. But Dogger still comes, sometimes in trousers, sometimes in a crocodile suit, slinking into the loft and her life like he were born to it.

And he's about to show up again.

Chapter One

Who am I?

Birdy mouths the words from the whiteboard, repeats them over and over in her head like a football chant.

Who am I? Who am I? Who am I? she asks.

But the answer always comes back the same: *I don't know.*

It's for her new school, Miss Higgins says. They're all to do it; write it in the booklet and stick in pictures of their family and their friends and all. They're to tell the teachers at the Academy what they were like as a baby, what they like to do now, and what they want to do when they're grown up.

Thing is, Birdy don't rightly know how to answer any of them questions. So by the time Miss Higgins has come round the class to peer over her shoulder she's only managed three lines:

Name: *Bridie Jones*
Age: *11*
Address: *27, Beasley Street*

She were going to put "Birdy", but then she'd have another load of nose-poking teachers and goggle-eyed kids to explain it to: how she were called it as a joke when she were little. How it stuck because of the birds. She's not sure she wants everyone knowing about that. Who else has pigeons, after all? No one in her class, that's for sure. And no one else has got a dead mam, neither.

"What about books?" suggests Miss Higgins. "You like reading, don't you?"

"Aye." Birdy nods, adding the word to the few she's got. 'Cause she does love stories. Has done since she can remember. Even since her dad stopped reading to her 'cause the words got too long, though he said it was 'cause he hadn't the time, what with tucking Minnie into bed and getting out on shift. So then she just told herself tales or stole Dogger's, or borrowed books from the library and read them out loud to the birds for their own bedtime. One about a flying carpet and a phoenix who lived in the fire; one about an orphan who lived with her own grandpa and the goats he kept in another kind of loft in the mountains; and one about a wizard in a land called Oz and a girl who flew to meet him in her very own house. That one she already knew, 'cause she'd watched the film on the telly with her dad once, snug under the musty crook of his arm so's she could hide when the flying monkeys screeched through the air. "There's no place like home," he'd told her then, "and don't you forget it." But that were before Sadie, and, besides, Birdy's not the one who needs reminding, she thinks.

"And what about some words that describe you?" Miss Higgins suggests.

Birdy can smell her perfume, hear her impatience. But her head's fluff, stuffed with nothing but feathers. "I can't think of any, miss," she replies.

"I can," smirks Casey Braithwaite. Birdy looks up, catching her mouth the word, "weirdo". And Laura Potter laughs on cue, *hunh-hunh-hunh*, like a monkey. Only not a magic flying one.

"That's enough, girls," says Miss Higgins. "Get on with your own work." She turns back to Birdy. "Try," she urges. It comes out in a sigh, thick with disappointment.

"I am," insists Birdy.

"Ask someone who knows you well. Your dad, or your . . . stepmum."

If Dogger were here, he and Birdy would laugh at that – at Sadie knowing anything real about Birdy, or wanting to. But this is school, and Dogger don't go to school. More's the pity.

"Want to see what I put?" Casey Braithwaite says, now that Miss Higgins has moved on. She pushes her booklet across the table towards Birdy.

Birdy hesitates. If she looks, Casey might call out, "Copycat!" If she doesn't look, Casey'll say she's stuck up. Stuck up and smelly, probably – she's said that before, after all. Birdy finds it hard to win with Casey. But maybe this time ... She leans over.

"'Intellectual'," she reads.

"That means clever," Casey announces.

"I know that," Birdy replies. *I'm not flaming stupid*, Dogger would add.

She carries on reading: *Intellectual. Inquisitive. Flexible.* A show-off, nosey and can do the splits, Birdy translates. And not one of these things can Birdy say about herself, so she's not going to borrow. But that don't stop Casey.

"Copycat!" she yells.

Birdy flushes, red as the rim of a pigeon's eye, pushes the notebook back. "I weren't, miss," she says. "I were just interested."

Miss Higgins raises an eyebrow. "Bridie, if you spent less time 'interested' in other people's work, and more time on your own, you'd be done on this page by now."

"Yes, miss," she replies.

Manjit Singh, sat opposite, pulls a face. But she can't tell if it's laughing with her or at her so she looks down, back to her almost-blank book.

She don't know why she's got to do it, anyway. Whose business is it but hers who she is? And, so strong is that thought, it flaps out of her mouth before she can catch hold of it.

"What's the point?" she yells. "Who cares how clever we think we are? They'll find out soon enough, any road."

Casey Braithwaite's eyes go wide and her mouth gapes like a baby bird waiting for worms.

Miss Higgins's lips tighten, so that when she speaks the words are small and sharp as stones. "Save your words for your work," she snaps.

Birdy's red cheeks darken to scarlet. 'Cause it's not words that's the bother, she knows enough of them – hundreds more than her sister, than her dad and Sadie, even – it's the facts that aren't so easy to pull out of the hat – the facts about Mam. Because how do you explain that even though you barely remember the shape or the smell of her, there's a hole in you that nothing fills, not Sadie's cakes that she plies you with, in place of kisses; not swimming with Minnie, 'least not now she can beat you at front crawl though she's barely four; not even Dad any more. Not now he's barely around because of the cabbing. If he got a proper job in an office, like Casey Braithwaite's dad, then it might be all right, 'cause at least he'd be back for tea, but who'd give him one of those when he stumbles over even baby-small words? When he can't even read *Dear Zoo*?

No, the only thing that fills the gap for a moment is Dogger.

And birds.

As soon as Birdy thinks of it – the hum and trill of them soft in the loft; the panicky flap when they're tossed on Cop Hill, thrown high into the air by her and Grandpa to give them a head start; then the whoosh and wheel when they work out which way's home – she feels the tight pull on her tummy slacken, and the white-knuckle grip of her fingers loosen round the blue biro. Safe, saved, she doodles pigeons and sings in her head while she waits for the bell, the birds, and the solitary loft.

And, just maybe, Dogger.

When she gets to the school gates someone's waiting, but it's not Dogger.

"All right?" asks Manjit Singh, his words having

to clamber over the fat wad of pink gum that nestles on his tongue. "Want some?"

He holds out a packet of Hubba Bubba and Birdy wonders what the trick is.

"It's not a trick," he says. "If that's what you're thinking."

"I'm not," she says, then reaches for a sweet, unwraps it quick, popping the gum in her mouth and pushing the wrapper into her pocket, where it sits with her lunch card and a hairband and a handful of seed.

"You going round your grandpa's?" Manjit asks as they set off. "You always do, after school. I've seen you. I live up the road from him. Is it 'cause your mam works?"

"She's not my mam," she says, half-wishing she'd never taken the gum now he's by her side, flanking her like he knows her.

"Who is she, then?" he asks, his feet one-two, one-two in time with Birdy's.

"Sadie. She's a mobile hairdresser," she tells

him. "Only she's got no car any more 'cause the engine went, so they come round ours and she does 'em in the kitchen."

"Does who?"

"I don't know. All sorts."

Manjit's like a fly, buzz-buzz-buzzing in Birdy's ear. She wants to swat him. Hopes he flies off of his own accord before they get near Grandpa's.

No such luck.

"Not my mam," he carries on, oblivious.

Oblivious, Birdy says to herself. That should be in Manjit's booklet. "No," Birdy agrees. "Not your mam. She's got sense."

Manjit blows a bubble, pops it. "What do you do at your grandpa's, then? Do you watch TV? I do, but just until my sisters get home. They only want to watch boring stuff. Do you do *Minecraft*?"

"Pigeons," Birdy says then.

"What, *Minecraft* ones?" Manjit says.

Birdy rolls her eyes. "No, real ones," she says. "He's got a loft. My grandpa, I mean. He keeps

24

'em in there. For racing, like. Season starts in a few weeks."

"Brilliant," Manjit says.

And it's like he means it, so Birdy says some more. Might as well, they've got two roads to go. "Loads, he has. But some's more special than others. Billy Bremner's the best."

"Like the old Leeds United player?"

"Aye," she says. "Only this is the fifth Billy Bremner now, rightly."

"What happened to the other ones?"

Birdy counts on her fingers. "Two died of old age, one got lost and one got eaten by Mrs Housden's cat."

"Poor beggar."

"Aye." Birdy thinks of the empty pen that night, her grandpa's face as he buried the bird behind the runner beans. She changed the subject. "I got my own and all," she says.

"Own loft?"

"Own bird. Marilyn. Only Grandpa keeps

her, 'cause we've not got a loft at home. My dad wouldn't mind one, I reckon — he used to love pigeons as much as me. Only Sadie says they're dirty. 'Rats with wings', she calls them."

"But they're not."

Birdy shakes her head. "No. 'Specially not my Marilyn. You should see her race. It's like she were born to it. All them birds flap-flapping, but she beats 'em all."

"Can I see her?"

They're outside Grandpa's house now and Birdy fidgets, wishing him away. "Shouldn't you be getting home?" she says, she hopes.

"It's four doors away. I'll only be a minute."

Birdy feels the tight pull on her tummy again. "I can't," she says. "Not just like that. I'd have to ask."

Manjit shrugs. "Maybe another time?"

It's not a rhetorical question. He's waiting for an answer. Birdy nods. "Maybe," she says. If she can trust him, she thinks.

26

Satisfied, Manjit pops another bubble and pulls the paper-thin pinkness back into his mouth with a flourish, as if it's gold not gum. "See you, then," he says.

"See you," Birdy replies. Because she will, won't she, at school. It's not a promise, not a definite "aye". And, happy with that, she clicks open the gate, clanks it shut, then clip-clops down the side return, straight to the bottom of the garden.

She thought he might be waiting for her – been sat there in the armchair with a pigeon in his lap. They weren't supposed to have birds in that side of the loft, that side were only for prepping and for thinking and for looking at Grandpa's certificates on the walls, but none of them stuck to the rule, not Dogger, not her and not even Grandpa. But today it's just the birds, cooing and shifting and busying themselves with bird business: the older ones plump and preening, their heads shining purple like oil on water; the young 'uns awkward, all wing and leg and a dusting of yellow fluff on grey, like pin mould on stale bread.

She might as well start cleaning them out, she s'poses. Grandpa can't do it, can he? Doctor Nesbitt's orders, on account of his pigeon lung. When he first told her that, Birdy imagined a growth of feathers inside him, like a fur ball in a cat that needed coughing up. He coughed all right, but all that came out was spit and curses. He's allergic, it turns out, the pigeon poo making his lungs red and sore so he's to stay away. So now she scrapes at the droppings for him, plops them in a pail and tips that into the bin at the back for emptying. Grandpa's friend, Harry the Horse, collects it once a fortnight for his roses. "Out of filth comes shining beauty," he told her once, only he didn't say "filth" he said a worse word, then told her not to repeat it. As if she would. She'd learned her lesson after doing a Dogger swear at the dinner table. "I'm just telling you what he said," she whined at the time, but Dad weren't having it, not in front of Minnie. "Or me,"

Sadie piped up. "I'm a lady, thank you very much." Birdy said nowt to that, but she'd heard her on the phone to her friend Donna, and none of that were very ladylike, thank you very much.

When she's done, she fetches a bird – Marilyn – slips her fingers round her belly, feels the feathers, soft as a pocket, presses her lips to the bird's head. "All right, Marvellous Marilyn?" she says, because she knows her birds, even if she don't know herself. "That's what you are, in't you? Marvellous. And magnificent. And deft. And daft and all." She laughs as the bird waggles and then poos on her palm. "Blimey," she says. "Thanks a bunch." She wipes it off on her school skirt.

"Don't let Sadie catch you doing that," says the voice.

She turns, though she don't need to, to know who it is. Grandpa.

"You're a star, Birdy Jones, did you know that?" he says, same as he says every day. "Don't know what I'd do without you."

Birdy eyes him with mild disappointment, but only for a second, 'cause if she can't have Dogger, he's next in line. "Well, you don't have to wonder, 'cause I'm going nowhere."

Grandpa nods, strokes Marilyn's head, and the top of Birdy's and all. "How was school?" he asks.

"It were all right," Birdy lies. Then changes her mind. "We've got to do a booklet, for big school. Say who we are and who we want to be."

"So who *are* you?" he asks. "And who *do* you want to be?"

"I dunno." Birdy shrugs.

Grandpa shakes his head. "Got to know where you come from to know where you're going."

A riddle, Birdy thinks. Another one. He always speaks in riddles, that or football talk.

"Was that Manjit Singh with you?" Grandpa asks then.

"What?" Birdy starts, flapping invisible wings. "How do you know?"

"No one's name I don't know round these

parts," Grandpa replies. He's puffed up, full of pomp and pride, like the cock of the walk. "You can ask him in next time, you know," he adds.

"No, you're all right," Birdy replies.

Grandpa's caterpillar brows climb up. "Because of Dogger?"

"Aye," Birdy says, quiet with guilt.

"Dogger might not always be about," says Grandpa.

"Why?" Birdy says, louder now, guilt given way to worry. "Where's he going?"

"Hey, hey, I'm just saying," Grandpa shushes her. "It don't hurt to have more than one friend."

Birdy keeps schtum to that. But he's right, there's no Dogger just now, she can feel it. There's a fat gap in the air, a space where he should be. He's far away today, on a field trip with his mam, maybe, like the time he went to the museum, or to Mars, he reckoned.

"I'd better get back," Birdy says, holding Marilyn out to Grandpa.

Grandpa nods but pushes the bird away. "Take her," he says. "Send her back with news of what's on the table for tea."

Birdy half-smiles again. "I will," she promises. And, packing the bird in a carry-box and her bag on her back, she trip-traps down the plank, up the garden path and off towards home.

Birdy bursts through the back door to find the kitchen half-full of Mrs Watts, pink face sweating through powder, bleached hair wound round rollers, and Sadie standing back like she's created a flaming masterpiece. Only then she catches sight of Birdy and, worse, what's under her arm.

"Christ on a penny farthing!" she yells. "Will you get that bird out of here? How many times?"

"I will in minute," Birdy promises. "Just, what's for tea?"

Sadie sticks one hand on her hip, holds a hairbrush in the other, like a gun. "Steak-and-kidney pie," she says. "Now shoo, love, get on with you." She points her weapon at Birdy, who shoos.

"Unhygienic." Birdy sits on the back step with a slip of paper and hears Mrs Watts moan, "Dirty. That's what."

"Don't pay them any mind," Birdy whispers to Marilyn. "You're not dirty. You're clean as a whistle. Cleaner than our Minnie and she lives in the swimming pool. Going to be a champion, she reckons, like Dad were." She thinks of Minnie then, goggle-eyed and sleek. If she lifted her vest and showed off scales Birdy wouldn't have blinked an eye.

"What about you?" Marilyn seems to coo.

"Maybe I'll be a bird," she whispers. "Like you. Fly over the Pennines and all the way to Manchester. Or London. That's where Dogger's going one day. Like Dick Whittington, he says." She wonders then if he's already gone and the thought sits like a cold seed in her stomach, souring it. "Or maybe I'll just stay with Grandpa."

She sighs, then writes, *Steak and Kidney so I wouldn't bother if I were you!* on the note and slides it under the ring on the bird's leg. Then, perching on the step, pigeon in her hands, she tosses her high into the air, her heart soaring and her soul feather-light, as she watches her bird wheel over the trees then, mind made up, swoop straight down the centre of Beasley Street and off to the loft.

Home.

Chapter Two

She finds out before she's supposed to.

It's because of the grate in the floor. It were
for heating, once, a chugging, clanking system
that Mr Noakes, their one-eyed landlord, ripped
out and replaced with radiators. Only he forgot
the grates, so now Birdy can hear things, secrets,
whispered down the phone or across the dinner
table when they think her and Minnie are asleep.
She knew about Dad getting sacked before he
told her. Knew when he'd thrown Mad Maxine
out for fooling about with Jimmy Quinn. Knew
about him and Sadie and all, moving in, getting

married. Heard her on the phone to Donna: "She'll get used to it. We both will." Then, Donna must've made a joke, 'cause Sadie laughed like a pig snort and said, "I don't know what goes on in her head, I really don't." And Birdy knew it were about her, and it weren't likely to be good.

Birdy stopped earwigging for a while after that, but this afternoon she's all ears, because Dad's been hovering about, fiddle-faddling with things and Sadie's all smiles and telling Birdy that she can go out if she wants, over to the shed.

"Loft," Birdy corrects her. "And you're all right." She goes to her room instead, lies on the carpet by the grate and listens.

It's Dad she can hear. "It's ideal," he says. "Three beds, big garden, just round the corner from your mam. Even got the garage converted so you could put the salon in there."

Birdy feels herself ruffle, like her wings are itching. Or about to be clipped.

Sadie squeals. "When can we see it?"

"We'll go Monday when the kids are at school. I'm not at work until two."

"I can't wait to tell Mam," Sadie says. "And Donna."

"Aye, well, just not the kids, not yet."

Too late, thinks Birdy. Too late for that. The cat's out of the bag now. The bird has flown.

She should swallow it down, she knows. Bury it deep inside, like all the other stuff she's not supposed to know about. But this news is too big, bulges out so she can't get a grip on it, and in the end all she can do is drag its bulk down the stairs and dump it in a heap in front of them, and see if they care.

"Blimey, Birdy," Dad says. "What have I told you about earwigging?"

"But is it true?" she asks. "Are we moving?"

Dad looks at Sadie, only Sadie bats it straight back to him. So he closes his eyes and sighs, deep and long, like he's digging for the right words, for any words. But all he can find is, "Aye, we are."

"Why?" she asks then. "What's wrong with here?"

"It's too small, love," Sadie says. "You know that."

"No, I don't," Birdy says. "We all fit."

"Not with—" Sadie begins, only Dad nudges her shut. "What?" she says. "She's got to know some time. Might as well be now. Better we tell her straight than she has to stick her ear to the wall."

"Tell me what?" Birdy asks, flapping like she's lost her perch, don't know which way to turn.

"The thing is ... " begins her dad. Only he don't have the words again, 'least not the right ones. Can never seem to find them.

Sadie can, though.

"We're having a baby," she finishes for him.

"What for?" Birdy asks. "You've already got one."

Sadie laughs, but Birdy reckons it's a lie of a laugh, a bitter spit, not round and happy.

"We've got two," her dad says then. "Minnie and you."

38

"I'm not a baby," Birdy says, taking herself out no sooner than he's slipped her in.

"I wasn't saying that." Her dad sighs.

"The point is," said Sadie. "There's not enough room here once there's three of you."

Birdy racks her brains, looking for words or stories that'll help. "It can go in with me and Minnie. There's room for a cot. Or we can get bunks."

Dad shakes his head. "You don't even like sharing as it is."

That's true enough, Birdy knows, but beggars can't be choosers. "I don't mind," she insists. "Or, once upon a time, they put babies in drawers. I read about it."

"Birds and books," mutters Sadie. "That's all you care about. No wonder your head's in the clouds. And I'm not putting any baby of mine in a drawer, I'm telling you that now."

"The new house has got a garden, Birdy," Dad tries. "A proper one. And it's nearer your new school—"

"And further away from Grandpa," Birdy interrupts, the truth of that hitting her *smack-bang* as she says it. 'Cause the other side of the city, where Sadie's mam lives, is miles away. Miles from Grandpa and the loft and . . .

She stops herself before she says his name.

"Your grandpa knows it's on the cards," Dad says. "Has done for a while. We can't afford to stay round here if we want somewhere bigger."

Birdy snatches at straws. "We could move in with Grandpa!" she blurts. "Or I could. Just me. It'd be all right. I know he'd have—"

"No!" Dad cuts her short. "That's not going to happen and you know it."

"But . . ." Birdy trails off, then finds the path again. "But who's going to do the birds? He needs help. You could drive me," she suggests, thoughts coming ten to the dozen, "like a job. Or I could get the bus."

"Don't talk soft," Dad says. "I haven't the time and nor will you."

"But – but … can we move the loft?" Birdy pleads, desperate now. "The new house has got a big garden – you said so yourself. Big enough for the birds."

"Over my dead body," says Sadie with a snort. "And your dad's. He's no more into them things than I am."

Birdy's eyes beg him to tell Sadie the truth – that he used to be, that he could be again. That it's only Sadie that's stopping him. But Dad's not looking, or else he's not good with eye words, neither, 'cause he just says, "That's enough," and tells Birdy to get back upstairs for a bit.

But Birdy's too angry for that, too angry to fit in her room, her whole body's hammering with it, and so instead of slip-slopping up the stairs, she pulls on boots, slams the back door behind her, and heads off, head down, to where she's wanted.

And this time, he's waiting.

*

"Shall we sing?" Dogger asks from his armchair throne, gold crown skew on his head.

Birdy sits, arms crossed, back to the wall, and shakes her head. She knows her voice will crack if she tries it. Besides, nothing's going to be right, whatever the three little birds claim, not any more.

"Story, then?" he offers. "I'll tell it. You can just sit there."

She nods this time, shuts her eyes, and lets him talk.

The story always starts the same: "Once upon a time." And ends the same: "And they all lived happily ever after." And in between the same princess is locked in the same tower by the same witch and the same prince comes to climb her hair and rescue her.

But Birdy never tires of it, it's part of her, always has been, she thinks, runs through her like blood. When he's done, and her heart's beating steady again, and her words are smooth and round as pebbles, she tells him what's what. About Sadie, fat with another baby, not sausage rolls, after all. About the new house with its three bedrooms. About it being far away. Too far for her to see to the loft every day. Or Grandpa. Or Dogger, for that matter.

But he don't seem to be thinking about that right now.

"So what'll happen to the birds?" he asks.

Birdy shrugs. "We'll have to let 'em go, or give 'em to Harry. He's been after Billy Bremner for ages. Or . . . " Birdy clutches at it. "You could do 'em. Help Grandpa, I mean."

Dogger shakes his head so the crown tips and topples. He picks it up and rams it back down, still the king. "He won't let me, will he?"

"Who, Grandpa?"

"Yer dad."

Birdy shakes her head, knows it's true.

"I'll think of something, though," Dogger promises, and stands to show he means it. Birdy smiles, but she don't rightly believe him. There's nowt to be thought of. Nowt that can fix a new baby on the way and a new house on the other side of town.

That's when Birdy sees his bottom half is clad in black tights and a tail that winds round his leg, all fluff and fur like the slink of a kitten. "Did your mam let you out like that?" she asks, wide-eyed as a bush baby, trying to imagine what Sadie would say if she tried it.

"Mam don't care," he says. "Well, she don't know. She's still in bed."

"How come?" asks Birdy.

Dogger shrugs. "The Black Death."

Birdy doubts it, but she doesn't say so. She can hold her tongue when she needs to.

"You'd better go, then," she says.

"You and all," says Dogger. "Or Sadie'll have your guts for garters."

Birdy knows it to be true, at least in word, if not in deed. "Aye," she says. "I will. I'll just do the birds first."

44

Dogger nods, and walks the plank.

"Don't forget, though," Birdy calls after him.

Dogger turns back, the sun a halo behind him. "Forget what?" he asks.

"A plan to help Grandpa!" Birdy's voice is dipped in desperation.

Dogger grins. "I know," he says. "I were only teasing."

"Bye, then," she says.

"Bye-bye, Birdy," he replies.

And then he's gone. Carried away by the air like a dandelion clock.

But he'll be back, Birdy says to herself, he promised, and with something more precious than a paper crown.

With a plan.

And she holds on to that thought as tight as she holds on to the memories of her mam, until it's hardened from no more than dust into a diamond.

Chapter Three

The hair's Sadie's idea. "A peace offering," she calls it. Only so far all it's brought Birdy is more grief.

"It's edgy," Sadie says as Birdy stares at the lopsided girl in the mirror – short over one ear, a curtain over the other.

Her dad's not so sure. "It looks half-baked," he says. "Like you just got bored and gave up."

"Tommo!" scolds Sadie. "All the girls at Rockefellers're getting it done. You'll see."

Birdy shudders as she thinks of the club. Of the queues of girls outside with too much make-up

46

and not enough clothes. All done up like fancy parrots, and the men strutting down the line, picking them out.

Not her dad, though. He just had to show up in his cab and they'd flit in like they were settling on a nest.

"Sorry, sorry," he says then and gets back to his telly – there's diving on, and him and Minnie are glued to the screen. Dad giving pointers, Minnie breaststroking across the coffee table in her cossie and goggles.

"You do like it, don't you, love?" Sadie asks.

"I s'pose," says Birdy, the best she can do. Only she pulls on a hat for the rest of the afternoon claiming her right ear's cold now.

But there's no hat to be worn at school in the morning. No hiding there.

She shuffles in amid the smirks and the whispers and the "omigod"s, sits, head down at the table. But even with her eyes on her exercise book she can feel Casey Braithwaite staring.

"Who did that to you?" Casey asks her, bold as brass.

Birdy wants the shiny lino floor to open up and swallow her like a sink hole, prays to a god she don't rightly know exists to make it happen, but God and the floor won't oblige, got better things to do. So, "Sadie," she mutters, hoping that'll do.

But it won't. It'll never do, not for Casey. "She should sack herself," Casey says, wallowing in Laura Potter's laughter that comes quick and loud and ugly, glowing with it almost.

"It's geometric," Birdy tries, Sadie's word awkward on her tongue.

"Geomental, more like," snorts Casey, scoring another point and a volley of *hunh-hunh-hunhs* in place of applause.

"That's what I said," lies Birdy, but Casey's not taking it, not letting her switch sides, that'd be too easy.

"You look like a headcase," she hisses.

"Girls!" Miss Higgins's voice cuts in, snapping

their gobs shut, and keeping them that way for the whole hour as she plays them a film about bees and how they hold the fragile world together like so much insect glue.

But at break there's no escape and they march in her wake, throwing insults like stones, words so lemon-sharp they seem to spit 'em. "Weirdo." "Headcase." "Bird Girl."

Birdy takes refuge behind the bins, where it's too stale-smelling for the likes of them. Watches them from afar – the boys strutting and swaggering like playground jackdaws, the girls like crows, waiting beady-eyed for carrion, for the weak or weak-willed to wander their way.

And that's where Manjit finds her.

"Want a Wotsit?" he asks.

Birdy, hungry from skipping breakfast, from running out the class too fast to get a snack, nabs one, uses it to clog up her gob and keep the tears inside.

"My favourite," says Manjit, licking orange dust from his fingers. "Then Monster Munch, pickled onion, then Skips, then crisps, any flavour, as long as it's not plain."

Birdy nods like she agrees, though she'd not have the Skips up there, not before crisps.

"I like it," he says then. "Your hair, I mean."

"You do not," she blurts, not sure if he's lying or laying the ground for joke.

"I do," he insists. "It's fancy. Fashion-forward," he adds, words that sound snipped from a magazine or stolen off his sisters.

"You don't think I look like a freak?" Birdy asks, still half-scared of the answer.

"Nuh-uh." He shakes his head. "But if it isn't 'you', you should pick something else."

Birdy wonders if he knows that she's lost, wonders if she can tell him. Maybe a sliver; a slip of the tongue she can claim, if he laughs. "I don't know what is 'me' rightly," she says.

But Manjit don't pull a face or pull away. "You'll work it out," he says. "Just got to find yourself, then you'll find the right hair."

He sounds wise, like a god or a guru. "Who told you that?" she asks.

"*Chat* magazine," he says and offers her another Wotsit.

She still hasn't found herself when she sees Manjit waiting for her later at the gate, ready to walk with her to Grandpa's.

"How about a bob?" he offers, as he scuffs his toes and drags his heels along Wardell Road, dawdling where Birdy would normally race, desperate for the birds.

Only today, she finds herself tripping on his questions. "What's a bob?" she asks, thinking of Billy Bremner, his head bobbing up-down, up-down as he spies her coming in with his seed.

"Sort of the same length all the way round," Manjit says, "like a bowl."

Birdy don't like the sound of a bowl. "No," she says, sure of one thing. "It's too short, anyway. Well, on one side."

She's managed a joke and Manjit laughs and she bathes in it like it's syrup.

Then he adds another drop.

"Can I have your mobile number?"

Birdy looks at him as if he might be the mad one, the headcase. "Not got one," she says.

"How come?" he asks.

Birdy shrugs. "Who would I call?"

"Your grandpa?" he tries.

She shakes her head. "We got the birds for that."

"You could call me," he says.

"I s'pose," she says, like it's nothing. But it's not nothing, it's a fat wodge of a thing, a fresh pink piece of bubble gum, like a jewel. 'Cause it were true what she said. Who would she call? She's got no friends besides the birds and Dogger, never has had. No need, she'd told herself, only even then she knew it were a lie.

Casey pretended once. Asked her to join in hide and seek at lunch with the rest of them. It weren't 'til two minutes before the bell rung and she were still behind the bins that she realised Casey had changed her mind, or never meant it in the first place.

Maybe this is a trick too, Birdy thinks. Maybe Manjit's going to spread something round at school, make her out to be odd. Only he don't seem like he's the sneaky sort. He don't seem like he's going to change his mind or has got owt to hide. If anything, he's as full of truth as Dogger.

And at that thought, Birdy smiles again, dripping in the sugar-sweet, so that when they're there, at the loft, and he says, "I'd like to see the birds," she says, "Go on, then."

"For real?" he asks.

Birdy nods, hesitant now that it's out there, suddenly scared of what Dogger might say. "It's Toss Day, mind," she says.

"What's Toss Day?"

"We go up Cop Hill," she explains, "let them out and give 'em a good long run home. Practice for racing, like.'

'Epic,' says Manjit.

Birdy nods. 'Aye, it is. You'd have to ask your mam if you can come, mind."

"Nah," he says. "She won't even notice. Out at work 'til six, and me sisters'll be glad to be rid."

"Come on, then," she says, clicking open the gate.

"Nice one," he says, as it clanks closed behind them.

Manjit wants to know it all, and so she shows him: how to talk to them, soft, like, but not baby talk, as if they understand every word and more besides; how to hold them, one hand cupped under their bellies, the other stroking, stroking the words in; and how to clean them out and all, scraping the poo into the pail, trying not to breathe, an invisible clothes peg on your nose. 'Til you got used to it, 'til the smell's just one of nature, not nasty at all.

And Manjit does as he's told; so eager is he that

by the time Grandpa comes to see who's who and what's what they've got the birds in their crates already.

"Blimey," he says. "Efficiency personified."

"What's that?" asks Manjit.

Grandpa sees him then. "All right, Manjit?" he says.

"Aye," Manjit replies. "Right as rain."

Grandpa nods. "Good at your job, it means. Both of you." He turns to Birdy, to her hair. "Sadie?" he asks.

Birdy nods and he rolls his eyes.

And that's all he's got to say on it, before they're packing the van, and packing themselves inside, ready for the ride.

The van's old, older than Grandpa, and just as creaky. Held together with gaffer tape and faith, he reckons. "Say a little prayer she can take the extra weight," Grandpa says as he flicks the switch and sends a judder of life, of breath, into her bones. "Big lad like you."

55

Crammed on the front seat, Birdy and Manjit look at each other and grin, both skinny as whippets, light as feathers, even with all the Wotsits and gum. And like that, tight as sardines, thick as thieves, they trundle through the back streets and then up, up the steep slope of Cop Hill and into the sky, the van grumbling, Grandpa humming, and the pair of them smiling like haircuts don't even matter.

God, or someone, has decided to listen, because they're up the top now, all of Leeds laid out before them, crates laid out on the bonnet.

"How do they know where to go?" Manjit asks.

"'Cause they're trained," says Birdy. "Grandpa trained 'em."

"Aye," agrees Grandpa, "And you, mind. You did your bit."

Birdy nods, remembering the mornings setting the crate on the landing board so's they'd get used to the air, to the look and smell of home, then watching them flap round the garden, sending tennis balls into the trees to stop them settling down, roosting. "They're only to perch here," Grandpa told her, slapping the loft.

"Could they fly to Manchester?" Manjit asks then. "Take a message to my cousin Jamal?"

"No." Grandpa shakes his head. "They only go one way."

"Which way's that?" asks Manjit.

Grandpa looks at Birdy.

"Home," she says. "They can only fly home."

One at a time they take the birds out of their crates. "We could just open 'em, let 'em all flap out," Grandpa says, for Manjit's ears. "But it's better to toss 'em."

"Give 'em a head start, like?"

"Aye," says Grandpa. "Show him, Birdy."

And she does. Marilyn in her hands, she lowers her down, ready.

"What's it Dogger says?" Grandpa asks, sending a prick of guilt needling into Birdy's mind.

But Dogger's not around, is he, so it's not her

fault Manjit's taken his place. "Death or glory," she answers.

"Aye," Grandpa remembers. "Death or glory. Go on, then."

One . . . two . . . three . . . Birdy counts in her head, then out loud, "Death or glory!" she cries, and high, high, she tosses her bird, so high she has to shield her eyes to see her, wings tilted into the sun.

"Death or glory!" repeats Manjit as he throws his own bird – a fat one-year-old called Gordon.

"Death or glory!" echoes Grandpa, sending Billy Bremner up to join them.

They watch, the three of them, their three little birds soaring and swooping over parched grass.

"Now what?" asks Manjit.

"Now," says Birdy, "we go home."

"And?" Manjit's impatient, hopping himself.

She smiles, watching the birds take one last dip and then head out, a line of them, back towards town. "And we wait."

*

Billy Bremner and Marilyn are already back by the time the van has chugged its way home.

"Champion," says Birdy as they peer at them pecking the seed that was waiting for them.

"Where's Gordon?" Manjit asks, his face taut with worry. "Is he stuck?"

"Might be distracted," says Grandpa. "Lot of cranes up and a new tower so he could be confused if he's lagged behind the others."

"Or a cat," mumbles Birdy, her words bleak and bare as the boards they're stood on.

"A cat?" asks Manjit. "Really?"

"Aye," says Grandpa, "It can happen. If they get lost and set down too soon. But I don't reckon it's that. We've just to wait, patient. He'll come."

Birdy hopes he's right, holds that thought tight as a pebble as time tick-tocks tick-tocks round, clocking up the minutes.

"Seventeen," says Manjit, checking his watch.

Then, the hand gone round, "Eighteen."

"Stop it," says Birdy. "He'll come."

Manjit looks at her, doubt on his brow.

But come he does, a flap and a thud and a tumble of grey through the trap, then calm as you like, as if he's only been gone a minute, not lost for twenty, he hops on to a perch and has his tea.

"That," says Manjit, "were magic."

"Aye," mutters Birdy. "Always is."

And soon, still fat with magic, and a phone number on a slip of paper in her pocket, she skips towards home. Her haircut, and Dogger, forgotten.

Then she sees it, a sign, stuck in the mud by the front wall.

FOR RENT

And – *puff!* – like that, the magic is gone.

Chapter Four

That sign were the start of it – the bother. Stood there, bold as you like, for all and sundry to see. Every step she saw it and every step it seemed to grow more steadfast, more cocky, more real. So when Birdy tramped into the kitchen it were already on the wrong foot, but she kept her mouth clamped, 'cause the words that wanted out were Dogger's ones, all swagger and swears. And she says nowt for an hour, not when Sadie asks her how her hair'd gone down at school and she wants to scream and slap and spit back; not even when Minnie shows her how she can dive off the top of the sofa and she bashes into Birdy's legs so hard she feels a bruise bloom, like a black rose on her thigh; not even when Stacey Perry from the pet shop asks after her blow dry, 'cause she's got Wayne taking her down Luigi's later and she wants to look a picture. "I said, what do you think, Birdy?" she repeats. "Cat got your tongue?" She raises an eyebrow that looks crayoned on.

Birdy just looks down at her homework and pretends to be glued to the booklet that's still only no more than a sentence long.

"Don't take it personal," says Sadie to Stacey. "I don't."

It's not until Dad comes in, snaffles the booklet out of her hands and says, "What's all this, then?" that she says so much as a peep. "It's for school," she mumbles. "The new one."

"'Who am I?'" Dad reads.

"I'm Minnie Rose Jones," says her sister. "And I'm going to be the first human girl to swim faster than a shark."

Dad laughs, full of the joys. Because of the baby, Birdy thinks, and because they're flip-flapping out of here first chance they get.

"What about you?" he asks Birdy. "Who are you going to be?"

And that's it. Birdy feels it work its way up, the sour seed, the ball of hard-done-by, coughs it out on to his lap. "How the flaming hell should I know?" she says.

"Birdy Jones!" snaps Sadie. "That is enough."

"She swore!" yells Minnie, delighted. "Dad, Birdy swore!"

"I know, all right!" Dad snaps and Minnie's miffed now, tears spilling silent over her red apple cheeks. But Dad en't got time for crying. He slaps the booklet down, so Birdy flinches like a fledgling. "What's up with you now?" he asks.

"I'm not . . . I don't . . . " she starts, words caught in her throat like a fishbone that can't be coughed up. "No one tells me owt around here," she says finally.

"That's not true," Dad says.

"It is so," she bats back. "I don't know anything. Not about now and not about before, neither."

"Before what?" asks Dad.

"Before . . . before Mam went," Birdy blurts.

Dad bristles, face paling. "You know enough."

"I know three things!" she squawks. "Three. That she had red hair. That she liked books. And that she's gone."

Minnie lets a sob out at that, a croaking thing that rattles through them all.

Dad takes no notice of either of them. "Nowt else I can tell you," he says.

And that's that. His gob is stoppered up. But not 'cause there's nowt, Birdy thinks, but 'cause he's holding something in like the top on a shook-up bottle of Coke.

"I don't even know who I am," she says, trying to jiggle the lid loose. "And I hate it. I hate all of you with your snipping and your swimming; all good at summat . . . all knowing what's what."

Dad turns to Sadie but she's having none of it. "Don't look at me," she says. "This weren't my idea."

Birdy don't know what the idea even is, so she shutters her ears and hears Grandpa in her head. *You got to know where you're from to know where you're going.*

But she doesn't know, does she, or only half of it. But even that – the Dad-shaped bit – don't seem to fit, 'cause when she looks in the mirror she can't make out his dark curls or his big lips or the ears he can wiggle to raise a laugh. He's all bold brush strokes and wide charcoal lines. But Birdy? She's fine traces of pale pencil; fine hair and thin lips and ears that sit stubbornly still. They must be her mam's, she s'poses, but when she tries to remember, all she can make out are fragments, torn bits of paper: a pearl earring in a pink lobe, a gap-toothed smile, the smell of biscuits and damp. All it adds up to is a blur, a torn-out page in her history book. Precious, mind, but still a blur.

"You were only a kid," Grandpa tells her when she tries to find more. "'Course you can't remember."

But Dad weren't. He were a grown-up before she were even born and he don't know or won't say. Too upsetting, he reckons. Though it's more for Sadie's benefit, she thinks. Once he whispered to her, "She were a miracle, your mam, you know that?" But then came the, "Don't tell Sadie I said so," that followed any mention of her. And now no one talks about before at all.

No one except Dogger. He's the one who listens, then tells her what's what. He's the one with all the answers. And the plans.

And so that's where she goes. Soon as she's said sorry, served her time stacking plates and washing pots and making promises not to say owt like that again. Then, when Sadie's back's turned, she pushes her lunchbox under the sofa and says she left it at the loft. She'd better go back and get it, hadn't she?

Sadie don't want her to go, says it's gone seven already and she's got school in the morning and, look at her, she's already in a onesie. But Dad says, "Let her," and Sadie huffs a sound that seems to say, "You're too easy on that girl. If she were mine she'd be straight to bed without supper or shut in the cupboard under the stairs."

'Least that's what Birdy hears.

But Birdy don't care. That cupboard's nothing, not compared to moving. Grandpa and the loft's all she's got and she'd do a whole month locked up if it meant keeping her birds, keeping Dogger, 'cause what's he going to do once she's gone? What's she going to do without him?

So, red boots on over blue onesie, she slams the back door behind her and sets off quick, not caring who sees her like that, not Mrs Watts, not Manjit, not even Casey Braithwaite. "Dogger!" She calls out to him in her head as she goes. "Dogger, you got to come."

And so loud are her silent prayers, so fat with

need, that he must've heard her all the way from wherever he lives, because when she gets to the loft, bursts through the battered plank door, there he is, the king on his throne, waiting.

But this time there's no crown and no wise words or wisecracks. This time he's got something mithering him before he can get to advising Birdy.

"Who's your boyfriend?" he asks her, his eyes black as birds'.

"What?" Birdy says, but it hits her – *smack* – soon as she's said it: Manjit. "He's not my boyfriend," she corrects him quick. "Not even a friend, not really." *Not yet*, she thinks. "He's just a boy." She crosses her fingers and her heart that Manjit can't hear her, though it might be true for all she knows, he might not like her that much, might just be after the birds, or bored. Or biding his time 'til he spreads stuff about her at school.

"He looked friendly to me," says Dogger, picking a scab on his knee, pretending that's more important.

Birdy sees him lift the dried edge up, sees the tempting pink underneath, feels the air on it, sharp and sore. "Were you watching?" she asks.

"Maybe," he says, and, changing his mind, pushes the crust back down again, letting it brew for another hour or two.

"Why'd you not say owt?" Birdy asks, voice full of wanting. "You could've come and all."

Dogger shrugs. "Two's company," he says, then clocks her proper. "He the one told you to get your hair cut?"

Birdy's hand flies up to her ear, tugs at the too-short bit. "No," she says. "That were Sadie. She said I needed a 'look'."

Dogger nods, understanding now. "It's a look, all right."

She drops her hand, defeated. "I know."

Dogger's got nothing to say to that, not yet, because something else is on his mind now, he's back to business. "What you here for, anyway? It's late for you."

69

Birdy sits on an upended bucket. "It's me mam," she says, words soft as fluff on a fledgling. "I – I don't know about her, not enough, anyway. And I need to. For school and . . . and for me. I don't . . . I don't feel full," she says. "Like there's a gap in me. Not when you're about," she adds quick, "just the rest of the time. And if I knew more about my mam, maybe I'd be all right."

"What does your dad say?" asks Dogger.

"He says, 'Don't be minding about that so much, Birdy. It's me and Sadie that matters now.' But he must remember, he has to."

"What about their story?" Dogger asks then, feet on the floor now, elbows on his knees so he's leaning right at her, listening hard. "He must know that, at least."

"What story?" asks Birdy, imagining one with wolves and witches, or through the wardrobe.

"The story of how they met." He leans back again, like he's waiting for her to tell the extraordinary tale.

But there's no tale to tell, not really, and the bits she knows are ordinary, dull, not diamonds. "She just got in his cab," she tells him, like Dad's told her. "A fare that went on after her stop." Like Sadie. And the one before her. And the one before her. "Then they were together, then they weren't, then she died, then Dad got me."

"What else?" Dogger urges, eager for information like a newborn chick for worms.

"Nowt," Birdy says, sullen as a wet Sunday. "Nowt more than I've told you, any road. Dad reckons that's all there is to tell."

"But he's got you," Dogger says, "So he must have other stuff and all. She'll not have just handed you over with no papers, no nothing."

A match flares in Birdy, the smell of sulphur sharp, the flame lighting up a fleeting memory. "What stuff?" Birdy asks. "What papers?"

"Your birth certificate," Dogger tells her, like he's stamped it all official himself. "Everyone's got one. Even me."

"Like for swimming?" asks Birdy.

"Aye," he replies. "Kind of. But just with your name and the names of who your mam and dad are. And there'll be mementos and all," he says, sounding the word out grand and long like it's treasure itself, so that Birdy shivers in its presence: *muh-men-tose*. "Photos and that," he adds. "From when she were young. From when you were born and all. In a shoebox, probably, like my mam's got, full of all my things – books and baby shoes, more besides. I bet that's where they are."

Another match flickers, this time lighting up a shoebox with shells and glitter on it, and papers inside that she were too little to read. But she's not seen that, not for a long time. Maybe Dad's got rid, like when Sadie gave him a makeover and he chucked out all his old-man clothes. Or Sadie's squirrelled it away out of sight.

A third match catches. "Sadie's got stuff in a sideboard," she says. "Letters and bills and the like." Minnie's certificates, she thinks, all stacked up straight, neat and satisfying, like Minnie is and all.

"So look," Dogger tells her, like it's obvious.

It *is* obvious. She's got to hunt. "I will," she says, buoyed now, babbling. "I'll look in there when I get back, or soon as they're out. I'll find it and bring it and we can work it all out, can't we. Me and you?"

Dogger nods. "Me and you," he says. "Like always."

"Aye." Birdy breathes out, long and hard. Dogger's come good again. So she lets herself wonder at something else. "Did you see the sign?" she asks.

"'For rent'?" he says, reading it off his memory. She nods.

"Aye," he says. "I saw."

"Did you think of a plan?" she asks when it's clear he's not saying owt else.

"Not yet," he says. "Too much on my mind. But I'm working on it."

"Yer mam!" Birdy bursts. "I'm sorry. Is she any better?"

"Oh, aye," says Dogger. "Top of the world today, my mam."

"What about the Black Death?" asks Birdy.

"Not any more," says Dogger. "Today she's dancing and singing, 'cause every little thing's . . ."

" . . . gonna be all right," finishes Birdy.

And maybe it is, she thinks to herself, when she's lying in bed that night. 'Cause somewhere there's a box of delights, a box all of her, and soon she'll be digging for treasure, soon she'll open it up and what wonders will be inside! Then she'll know everything she needs to know – where she comes from, and where she's going.

Even if it is only the other side of town.

Chapter Five

It's five days before she even gets near to the sideboard.

Tuesday, she has to mind Minnie in the bath, holding the stopwatch while Minnie holds her breath underwater. She's told Minnie swimming's not like that, but Minnie says what would Birdy know? She don't even like the water. And Birdy can't argue with that.

Wednesday, its parents evening so she has to sit in the stale school-dinner smell of the hall with her dad and Sadie, waiting for Miss Higgins to call their turn. "You can sit with your friends, if you like," Sadie tells her. But there's only Laura Potter in line so she says, "You're all right," and carries on kicking her plimsolls at the parquet floor. Miss Higgins tells her dad she's a quiet one, that she could do with speaking up more. Sadie says she don't have that trouble at home. Miss Higgins says, "Well, she's bright as a button, that's the main thing," and shows them a poem Birdy wrote about the war, which Dad pretends to read, nods and says, "Aye, that's nice," even though it's about guts and grim death. Sadie just rubs her belly and pulls a face, says, "We should get going. Baby's sat right on me bladder."

Thursday, Sadie's in the sideboard herself, fiddle-faddling through drawers looking for pieces of paper for the new landlord. Birdy offers to look for her, and Sadie, oblivious, smiles, but then sucks the good away by saying if she wants to help she can make her a nice brew, only just the one sugar, 'cause the baby's getting fat.

And Friday she's up Cop Hill again with

Manjit. She'd not expected that. Thought he'd have blabbed before then about her and the birds; told Casey Braithwaite what a weirdo she was, like Casey don't already think that, anyway. But he'd zipped his lips in class and not asked about the birds all week, until they were walking home from school that day. She were going to say no, 'cause of Dogger, but Grandpa were waiting at the gate and just handed him the crate and Manjit grinned and popped his gum and told them how he'd been reading up on it on the internet, how a pigeon nearly won World War Two by taking messages to the Americans and how they've got no gallbladder. "What's one of them?" Birdy asks him. "I don't know," he replies. "But they en't got one." Pockets full of penny chews and a head full of facts, that's Manjit, she thinks. But he's all right, whatever Dogger reckons.

So Saturday's first chance she gets to look for the box. Dad's in bed, out like a light still 'cause he's topsy-turvy from the Friday night shift – the preening, pecking hens and swaggering stags, singing and swearing and falling asleep on the back seat, so he says. So Sadie's had to take Minnie up the pool herself and none too pleased, she is. She's got two sets of highlights booked for the afternoon and she could fancy a lie down herself. Up all night that baby were, like it were on the dance floor of Rockefellers itself.

"Going to be a right little mover, I'll warrant," says Sadie.

"Just like his mam," adds Dad, and Sadie smiles at that and lets him kiss her right on the mouth with his tongue and everything, just 'cause he said nice stuff.

So Birdy's glad when he trip-traps up the stairs, so she don't have to see any more of that.

"Sure you don't want to come with us?" Sadie offers.

But Birdy's bristled, ruffled up rigid and itching to get a move on with the plan, so she just shakes her head and counts silently.

One . . . two . . .

"Suit yourself," Sadie says. "Only don't say I didn't offer."

Three . . . four . . . five—

And at that the front door slams shut and Birdy's off to find the box, and herself. A pirate, she is, Anne Bonny; or Mary Anning, pioneering archeologist, digging for buried treasure. The first drawer is all bills and bits of paper with prices and names and numbers. Nowt for Birdy. Next is photos – paper ones, printed out proper and kept in folded-down packets. Dad in his trunks, sleek as a seal, with a trophy in his hands and a smile she en't seen for a long time. Sadie in school uniform with a right cob on – and gob on her and all, Birdy wouldn't wonder; Sadie with a crayon-red clown mouth of lipstick, out dancing on a Friday night; Sadie, sweaty-haired, with a baby in her arms: Minnie.

Birdy's in some photos, awkward and gawky, staring straight-faced at the lens, or away over the shoulder of whoever's snap-snapping, probably looking at a bird. There are no pictures of before, though, before she come to live with Dad, or before Sadie moved in with them. So she folds them all away in their packets and pushes that drawer shut, opens the next. But they're all the same – all full and empty at once, brimming with memories – mementos – but not the right ones. Not hers. And none of them in a shell-covered shoebox. Maybe that's her mistake, she thinks. A shoebox wouldn't fit in a drawer, it'd be in the attic, more like, or the shed. If it even exists, that is. That last thought sits there, the words hanging in the air like they're lit up in neon, all glowing and poking a finger at her, as if she's as stupid as Jason Blake in her class, who thinks the sun gets switched off at night.

She hears her dad shift in bed: a cough and a creak on bare floorboards through paper-thin walls. She's running out of time and places to look. "Where is it, Dogger?" she pleads out loud.

But Dogger's not listening, or so she reckons, so

she goes to shut the cupboard door, an angry slam
planned, and that's when she spies it, poking out
from a crack down the back, slipped out of sight,
or pushed there. A fat brown envelope, no shells,
no glitter, but one word – a name – in her dad's
staccato hand.

BIRDY

And her wings unfurl and she almost squawks
with it.

She peels it out careful, so careful, as if it might
fall from her fingers and – *whoosh!* – disappear, or
crumble to nowt but dust. And when she shakes
out the contents, gossamer-light, she feels for all
the world like it's a crate she's opening, letting
loose those magnificent birds to soar up and
swoop and show the world just who they are.

And maybe it is. For out plops a picture, face-
down, with black ink, joined up this time, looping
out beautiful words.

Eating for three
Love always, Fitz

Then at the bottom there's a name – *Will
Fitzsimmons* – and three more words: *Write to me!*
Birdy wonders if he did.

Who did?

Heart patter-pattering, Birdy turns the photo
slowly over. And there! Right there is her mam!
Red hair and green eyes, just like she were told.
Face crammed with cake and her bare belly, fat
with it and more besides, because in there, in
that taut barrel, is a baby – Birdy. Birdy traces the
shape of her mam's face, strokes her hair; sees that
the same brush that painted her plaits copper has
spattered her skin with freckles, and Birdy feels
her own fingers fly to her nose as if to check hers
are still there, not lost or faded.

This is Mam, she says to herself. This happy,
jam-faced lady, sprawled on a bank on a sunny
afternoon. She's not a blur any more, not

fragments; she's painted clear and bright and in glimmering, gaudy colour. There's a man next to her. Not Dad. Fitz, she reckons, brown-haired and bare-chested, his tongue stuck out so she can see a wodge of cake sponge in his mouth too. Birdy wonders then if it's birthday cake, and if so, whose, and she touches her mouth, then her mam's bare belly to feel herself inside; feels a rush of happiness through her that sends her head spinning and ringing. Like she's on the waltzer at the fair and might throw up if she stays on any longer. But she wants to stay on, has to, 'cause the gap's still there, there's still something missing, and so she shakes the envelope a second time. Only nowt comes out. For a moment she falters, worried that's all there is of her mam, and her, and not much it amounts to. But then, determined, like the last lick of the baking bowl, she pokes a finger under the flap, wiggles it, worm-like. There! She can feel it, a crisp edge of almost-card, and almost as big as the envelope itself. Pincering it, she pulls, and then – *ta-dah!* – it's on her lap, like a rabbit from a hat.

But it's no rabbit. Birdy knows what this is – this is her birth certificate, like Dogger told her. A certificate just for being her! And look who she is:

Bridie Eleanor Henderson.

Now that were a name she hadn't reckoned on – a big name, bulging with purpose and fancy. No Jones for her, 'cause her mam weren't ever married to her dad. Only where did the Henderson bit go? It's been stolen away. Taken right off her. Like someone handed her shiny-wrapped sweets and then snatched them all back. Only who did the handing and who did the snatching? She reads on, searching for the line:

Mother: Bonnie Henderson.

Bonnie. Bon-nee, she sounds it out, but soft, so's Dad won't stir.

Occupation: Student.

So she were still at university, Birdy thinks. Not even a grown-up, not really. But Dad's forty-seven now, so he must've been — Birdy subtracts eleven, counts down in her head — thirty-six then. Thirty-six! That's a whole — she counts again — fifteen years on Bonnie, on her mam; more than Birdy's lived yet.

She looks for her dad's name, then. For Thomas Joseph Jones. Scans up and down and up again. But something's wrong, 'cause each time comes up bare. It says, Father, all right, she can see that. But next to it, instead of a name — his name — there's a single word.

Unknown.

Birdy feels funny. Faint. Like the world's stopped turning, but spinning too quickly all at the same time. She clamps her hand over her mouth in case she's sick, or screams burst out, but nowt comes. Instead there's a thin, insipid silence as the fullness she felt from the photograph drains away and the one thing she knew about herself is rubbed out as if it were no more than spidery pencil in the first place.

So that now, instead of knowing exactly who she is, she is no more than a blur of a bird, a distant thing, lost and alone, and no idea which way is home.

Chapter Six

She sits and thinks and sits and thinks only she can't make head nor tail of it and she just feels sicker. She needs to get out, to get to the loft or up into her room, where she can disappear into a book. But by the time she's realised that she don't get a chance.

"Birdy?"

She hears the scrape of the key in the front door, the dull creak as it opens, Minnie's gabble filling the hall. She scrabbles to put the certificate away, pushing it carelessly into the envelope and that into the cupboard. The photo, though – that she keeps, popping it into her pocket, feeling its crinkle and crack as she stands.

"What you been up to, then, love?" Sadie's stood in the doorway, red-faced from the heat of the pool and the puff of pregnancy; chlorine smell drifting from the towel bag in her hand.

"Nowt," Birdy says quick, her own face pinking like prawns in a hot pan, holding Sadie's gaze so it don't slip to her trousers and see what she's got hidden.

But Sadie's got other things on her mind. "Yer dad up yet?"

Birdy shrugs.

"Flaming hell. Tommo!" she yells upstairs.

She hears another cough and a creak and then the thud, thud of feet and her dad lumbers down the stairs, bleary-eyed and sweat-smelling, still not showered, though he pulls Sadie in for a kiss, anyway.

"Get off," she says, but smiling. "You stink."

Birdy stands, eyes agog at them, at him, this father who's not.

Dad clocks her. "What's up with you?"

Birdy shakes her head. "Nowt," she says again, two lies in two minutes. But he's told more, she reckons, must've, if that bit of paper's true. She watches him then, plodding to put on the kettle, his wide swimmer's shoulders, his one-time tight drum of a tummy gone to fat. He's a great lummox of a man, nowt bird-like, Birdy-like about him at all. But then why would there be if there's no blood connecting them?

She keeps watching him all morning: spooning sugar into his cracked Leeds mug; lying on the sofa with his feet up, picking fluff from his belly button; at lunch as he sucks soup off dipped bread. Her eyes flit from his hands to his hair to his lips, half the time trying to join the dots, to see how she fits with him, half-searching for other answers: if he's not her dad, why's he got her? Was she left in a dustbin, or on the doorstep in a cardboard box? Did he kidnap her?

Does he wish he'd never bothered now?

Dad catches her staring. "Eat up," he says, pointing at her bowl, still swimming with soup.

"Not hungry," she mumbles and that's not a lie. Her tummy's a tangle of half-hitches, so sick does she feel. 'Cause she can't work out why she's here, don't feel like she fits, not even with him. Oh, she loves him, all right, still feels that in the bones of her. Only she don't know how or why or if she even wants to any more. She shifts in her seat; hears the crackle of the photo in her pocket. "Can I get down?" she asks.

"To do what?" asks Sadie. "If you're not well you want to get to bed."

"I'm all right," Birdy lies. "Just not hungry."

Sadie sighs. "Well, if you need a job you can start going through your stuff. Work out what's for keeps, what's for charity and what's for chucking. Three piles," she emphasises, as if Birdy can't count. "Saw it on the telly and it's a right good system."

Birdy feels herself go rigid. She'll not be doing that, not yet, not *ever* if she gets her way. If Dogger comes up with a plan, that is. "Birds," she blurts out. "I got to do the birds."

Sadie's face sinks. "Oh, Birdy," she says with a sigh. "You've got to stop with that. And your grandpa wants to be thinking on and all. Not long now 'til we move, he knows that."

"Sadie," her dad – the man who says he's her dad – scolds.

"What?" says Sadie. "It's true, in't it? He's got to sort them. It's for his own good. For his health."

"Aye, but—"

"But nothing." Sadie's teeth are gritted so the words have to fight to get out. "Someone has to talk sense into him. And this one." She nods at Birdy.

"I'm not stupid," Birdy protests.

Dad shakes his head. "No one said you were, love."

"She did." Minnie points his spoon at Sadie.

"I did not," says Sadie, pushing Minnie's spoon back into her bowl before it drips red soup on the scratched wood of the table. "And you know it. Stop sticking words in my mouth."

"Sorry," says Birdy, and she almost is. Almost. "So can I go, then?" she asks, one last time.

"Aye," her dad tells her. "Go on."

And so she goes, quick, before he changes his mind or Sadie changes it for him.

She's hoping to see Dogger as soon as she gets there, but what she gets is Grandpa, sat out on the garden bench, arms stretched and sunning himself, though it's barely April.

"All right?" he asks as she stamps past.

"No," she says back, and carries on clomp-clomping up the plank and into the dark of the loft.

She spies the empty chair and sighs, but the musky air is alive with hum of birds busying themselves, and, seeing the pail, she grabs it and starts on the *scrape, scrape, scrape* of spade on sanded wood.

Grandpa gives her a minute before he follows her in. "*Cooling-off time*," he always calls it. "Time to ponder your problem and let it shrink down from the mountain you see, to the molehill it probably is." But it's going to take longer than a minute to shrivel this one down to any size.

"Want to give us a clue?" he asks her.

Birdy shrugs.

"All right," he says. "A guessing game, then. Is it . . . Sadie again?"

Birdy shakes her head.

"School, then? That whatsername – Braithwaite girl – been giving you a hard time?"

Birdy hesitates, shakes her head again.

"Okay. So not Sadie, and not school. And it can't be your Minnie, because she might be a minx at times but she's never caused bother this big." He scratches his head, exaggerates it like he's trying to find a flea as well as the answer. "Bingo," he says then. "It has to be your dad. Only a great hulk could make you sulk like this."

Birdy's head moves not one millimetre.

"So, your dad it is. What's he done this time?"

Birdy thinks hard. She could tell him what she's seen, she s'poses. Ask him for the truth of it. Only what if he don't even know the truth? Don't know about 'Unknown'? What then? Maybe his heart would go the way of his pigeon lung, race so fast it gives out and he falls, smack on the floor.

So Birdy stays stoppered up, just carries on scraping poo into a bucket.

"He loves you, you know," Grandpa says after a while. "I know he don't always make a song or dance about it. Maybe he don't even say it out loud, I don't rightly know. But ever since the first time he saw you, he's loved you."

Birdy feels strings on her heart plucked, one, two, three. Has to wait a second for them to stop vibrating. Stares instead at Grandpa, at his great fat hands, nails yellowed with nicotine and knuckles swollen with age; sees her own hands, thin as bone, thin as Gretel's chicken claw she pokes through the cage. How can they be related? How can any of him be in her? Maybe all they got in common is birds, no more than that, and they're flighty, flapping things that only live for a few years.

"You're not supposed to be in here while I'm doing this," she says eventually. "You know that."

Grandpa nods, sighs. "Right you are, then." And out he goes, slow as a loris, but sure.

Birdy waits for the door to close and the gloom to fold in, but as soon as the wood clacks in its jambs, a sliver of silvery light falls across the filth of the floor and something – a spirit – sneaks in.

Dogger.

Birdy turns to see him, sunk suede-headed into the chair, his hair shorn shorter than short like one of those poor kids in the camps in the war.

"What happened to you?" she asks him.

"Nits," he replies.

Birdy flinches, remembers the tight teeth of the comb tangled in her hair; remembers Sadie's

95

suggestion: "It'd be easier to shave it all off," she said. "Save us both the bother." But Dad had stopped her, sided with Birdy. That time.

"My dad's not ..." she blurts, but stops before she finishes the sentence.

"Yer dad's not what?" Dogger asks.

"He's not ... my dad," she manages. "'Least he might not be."

It all comes out then, a tumble of words like toppling blocks: the slipped-down envelope, the certificate, the certainty she was going to find something, and that word – that word that's changed everything, tipped her world so everything's skew, as if she's looking at it now in a fairground mirror or the back of a spoon.

Dogger listens and then says a swear when she's done.

"Aye," Birdy replies, only managing one word because the tears are coming now, pushing their way out in front of anything else she wants to say. The one thing she wants to say.

But Dogger sees it, reads the question that's being held in. "So, if he's not your dad, then who is?"

Birdy wipes her eyes, swallows a sob before it finds its way out. "How do I know?" she says. "Could be anyone."

"Well, not anyone," says Dogger. "Not Denny Dawson, 'cause he's black, and not Mrs Watts's brother Neil, 'cause he likes men, but apart from them, loads of people."

"Exactly."

"My dad's a rock star, did I tell you that?" Dogger says then.

Birdy's brow creases. "I thought he was a jewel thief. That's what you said."

"Did I? Maybe he's both. Maybe he's King of China."

"China en't got a king. It's got a president."

"Whatever. Anyway, it's not my dad we've to worry about. It's yours. *He* might be President of China, for all you know."

Birdy looks down at herself. "I don't look very Chinese," she says.

"No," agrees Dogger.

Birdy feels dizzy, like her body's still catching up with her brain. Or the other way around. "Anyway, maybe he is my dad really, but it just don't say it on the certificate. I don't know. I don't know owt any more."

"Not your arse from your elbow," says Dogger, then grins, and as he does, it tugs at the corners of her mouth, twitches them up to mirror his.

"I like your hair," she says.

"Good, in't it? Like a velveteen rabbit, my mam says. Here." He lowers his head. "Feel it, go on."

She does as he's told her, and his mam's spot on, it's soft and stubbly all at once.

"You want to be doing yours," he says then.

Birdy pulls her hand back. "What?"

"Your hair, same as mine."

"But . . . I've not got nits," Birdy says.

"Nor have I," Dogger replies. "Not now."

Birdy touches her own lopsided mop, tangled and straggled with two-day-old dirt. The thrill of it – of a smooth rabbit head – catches her like a wave, and she's powerful as the sea itself. She can't stop the move, can't work out who her dad is, let alone herself, but she can do this, show Sadie she's not her walking, talking Girl's-World head, nowt more than hair to experiment with. "Will you come with me?" she asks.

Dogger shrugs. "Not allowed round, am I? Not after last time."

Birdy feels herself falter, pulls herself up by her bootstraps. "Fine," she says. "Give us ten minutes."

Sadie's in the kitchen with a trolley full of tools and Deborah Dooley with her hair all folded in tinfoil. "Shut the door!" she yells as Birdy comes bursting in.

"I'll only be a minute," Birdy replies.

"Born in a barn," Birdy hears her mutter, and hears the slam as Sadie shuts it herself.

Maybe I was, Birdy thinks to herself as she flies

up the stairs to the bathroom cupboard, reaches past the jars of goop and God-knows-what to get Dad's clippers, stuffs them in her rucksack, pegs it back down, past the makeshift salon.

"Door!" Sadie yells again. But Birdy is gone, flying straight back to the loft like her very own Marilyn, fast and true.

"You got them?" Dogger asks.

"Aye." She gets out the gleaming clippers, unplugs Grandpa's radio and plugs them in its place.

"Give us them here."

Birdy hands them over, glad of it.

"Sit down, then," Dogger tells her. "So I can see proper."

Birdy does as she's told, sinking into the green armchair, her skinny arms stretched along the rests, bracing her for what comes next.

"It don't hurt," Dogger tells her. "Promise."

"Go on, then," she says, her feet fidgeting half with fear, half with want. "Get it done."

"Right you are."

Dogger clicks the switch, bringing the clippers to life, the waspish buzz sending the birds flapping for a moment before they and Birdy settle to the sound.

"Oh!" Birdy jumps as his hand touches her, and something else – cold, saw-mouthed metal.

But Dogger don't reply, stays silent as he moves the machine to and fro, to and fro, buzzing her skull and sending tendrils tumbling into her lap. Birdy grabs one, holds it up to the light and sees red-gold glint in the sullen brown, feels a quick prick of guilt as she thinks about the photo of her mam. "You've got lovely hair," Sadie always used to say to her. "If only you'd let me do something with it." And that thought swallows the guilt and smacks its lips, 'cause she's doing something now.

"There." Dogger turns the clippers off and the room swells with a sudden silence. "Done," he says.

Birdy can't see herself, but she can feel her hair,

like Dogger's, soft as suede, and, underneath it, her skull a perfect egg. It feels like freedom. It feels . . . like her.

"Birdy?"

Startled, she turns at the not–Dogger voice, sees Grandpa in the doorway, arms dangling, mouth hanging open. "It were Dogger's idea," she says quick.

Grandpa closes his eyes and shakes his head; opens them again, sees her still there. "I don't think Sadie's going to give a hoot whose idea it was, do you?"

"Well, I like it," she says, back up like a cat.

"I didn't say I didn't like it, did I?" Grandpa says. "Just it's a . . . surprise, is all." He comes closer so she can smell the meat pie and tobacco of him. He's not meant to smoke, that's doctor's orders and all, but he has a pipe sometimes. "A treat," he calls it. "Life's worth nowt if you can't have a treat." But he has it when he's needing cheer, when he's mithered.

So he must be mithered now.

"You want me to come with?" he asks. "Tell 'em I done it, not you?"

Birdy shakes her head, air cold on both ears now. "I'll be all right," she says.

"If you say so."

Birdy does say so. But saying isn't believing. And believing isn't being, she knows that.

Sadie cries, actually cries, when she sees her.

Only 'cause I can't be your flaming guinea pig any more, Birdy thinks to herself, but she don't say it, 'cause Dad's eyes are black.

"You look like a boy," Minnie says.

"I do not," Birdy replies. "Girls have short hair."

"Not me," says Minnie, swinging her own blonde ponytail so it flaps her cheeks, *swish-swash*.

"Who told you to do it?" asks Dad. "Were it a dare?"

"No one," Birdy insists. "It were my idea. Mine and . . . " She trails off, hoping he won't notice, but it's too late, Dad's clocked it.

103

"Yours and whose?"

Sick of lies, Birdy blurts it: "Dogger!" she says. "It were me and Dogger that did it. All right?"

But it's not all right, 'cause Dad's face gets red and he slams his hand down on the table, so hard it slops Minnie's milk and sends it pooling white on the floor, sends her bleating into Sadie's lap.

"Go to your room," he says to Birdy. "Now."

"Tommo," Sadie whispers. "Don't."

But he does. "Now!"

Birdy don't bother arguing, just turns tail and stamps, left–right, left–right, to the hammer of her heart. Out the kitchen, up to her bedroom she goes, and flops face-down on to her bed where she can sob into her pillow.

"I don't care what Sadie says," she says to herself. "She's not my mam. She's not in charge of my hair or owt else." Each thought sends another cry heaving through her. "Don't care what my dad thinks, neither, 'cause . . ."

He's not her dad.

She breathes deep, trying to take in enough air to stopper up her sobbing, to slow down and sort out her head, 'cause she needs to think straight now, work out a plan.

She thinks about him then. Not the glowering tower of the man in the kitchen but her real dad. Sees in her mind a smaller, smiling version, one that reads books and knows words, and don't drive a taxi that keeps him out all hours so he's not got the time for anything but sleep and swimming. One who reads to *her*, listens to her and all. Puts her above all else. And her real dad wouldn't have a Sadie, 'cause he'd still be too in love with her mam.

She turns in bed, pulls the photo out, trying to see through the salty blur: her mam, happy, 'cause she's got cake and she's got Birdy in her belly and she's got . . .

Birdy squints, sees him, sees the truth.

She's got Fitz. Will Fitzsimmons, sat right next to her, hand on her leg like they belong together.

They did belong together, because – Birdy clutches at it, before it flaps away – he's her dad.

Soon as she's said it in her head she knows it to be true. That Fitz – the man in the picture – is her real dad, and so she has to find him. Because he won't get mardy over her hair; won't make her move over the other side of town; won't have other kids or another wife, all he'll want is Birdy, and for her to be happy.

And happy for Birdy = birds.

Yes, if she can find him, then she can save the birds and all. They can build a loft together, a proper one, like Grandpa's, but better, even: bigger perches and a flypen all the way round for exercise and separate rooms for the eggs and the fledglings.

And just like that, her future's fat with promise and possibility, and a new name – Birdy Fitzsimmons – and she makes a vow, there and then, to find him. She don't rightly know how, but find him she will.

Then she'll know who she is.

Then the song will be true.

"Then every little thing will be all right," she imagines Dogger saying.

And with the song in her mind, like a lullaby, she lies on her back on her Superman duvet and waits for her new life to begin.

Chapter Seven

"Oh. My. God."

Casey Braithwaite's voice slaps her *smack-smack-smack* before she's even through the gates.

"She looks like a right mentalist," Casey carries on. "Don't she?" she adds, elbowing Laura Potter who blurts out an, "Aye," as if she'd forgotten it was her job to agree.

The not-even-whispers trail her across the playground as Birdy marches past, hands in pockets, head down, but she says nowt, don't even flinch, 'least not on the outside. Not when Casey says she's probably got cancer and scrapes her chair to the left in case she catches it; not when Kyle Johnson laughs so hard snot flies out his nose; not even when Miss Higgins clocks her and her mouth drops so she looks like she's catching flies. They don't matter, none of them, 'cause soon as she's found him – Fitz – she'll be long gone, and Miss Higgins and Casey and Sadie and all of them will be no bigger than ants, so small she could squash 'em.

"Can I touch it?"

Birdy whips round, startled, as Manjit plops down in the seat next to her, the seat that's been spare since Birdy can remember.

"I s'pose," she says, aware still of all the others' eyes on her – on them. "If you want."

He does want, and Birdy sits rigid as his thin fingers reach out and settle on the top of her head, as they push down on the stubble and swirl it slow and smooth, slow and smooth, like they're stirring a cake, or stroking an animal.

"Mad," he says, his hand still on her head. "I love it."

Me too, Birdy thinks, but doesn't say it. *Me too*.

"Bridie and Manjit," Miss Higgins calls out. Birdy feels her face flush, pulls her head away so Manjit's hand is left hovering in space on an invisible dog. "Weekend's over. Manjit back to your seat, please."

But Manjit's got other ideas. "I'm all right here," he says, cool as a cat.

The class falls pin-drop silent and twenty-seven hearts beat a fraction faster, waiting for Miss Higgins to snap, to put his name on the board for bad behaviour, for him to lose his golden time. Birdy feels it too – leg-jiggling anticipation – like the moment before a bird comes home . . . if they come home.

This time he does, he lands swift and neat.

"Well, I don't see why not," Miss Higgins says.

And, while twenty-six mouths sigh in silent disappointment, Birdy lets herself breathe again, relief brief but syrup-sweet. Because, just for now, Manjit's a force field or cloak of invisibility against them; she can hide in its folds, push the rich fabric in her ears and pretend they're not there – the Caseys and Kyles. Until she's so far away she won't hear them even if they trumpet their scorn.

"There you go." Miss Higgins carries Manjit's tray over for him, her eyes still fastened on to Birdy's head like it's got glue on, or glitter.

"It's a brave thing," Miss Higgins says then. "It says something about you."

"What's it saying?" Manjit says, asking Birdy's question for her.

Casey's mouth don't move but Birdy hears her thinking: "That she's a headcase."

But Miss Higgins thinks different. "That you're bold," she says. "Audacious."

"What's that mean?" Birdy asks.

"Look it up," Miss Higgins tells her. "That's one for your booklet."

Birdy nods a promise. But it's fast forgotten with Manjit beside her, and her real dad somewhere, somewhere out that window.

*

111

The internet were Manjit's idea. She'd not been going to ask him for help – not been going to tell him about her dad at all. But the photo poked out her pencil case when she were lending him her red gel pen and he wanted to know who they were and why she had a picture of them, and were they going in her booklet and a hundred other questions. So in the end she told him. Not right then, not with Casey Braithwaite earwigging, but after school, as they walked up Montgomery Road, cheeks fat and tongues red with aniseed balls.

"So your mam's dead?"

Birdy nods.

"And your dad – Mr Jones, I mean – he's not your dad, after all."

"That's right," she answers. "'Least I think not."

Manjit crunches down on his gobstopper, pondering, the same thought that swells Birdy's brain, makes her head hurt with it. "So why's he got you, then?"

"I don't know."

"Maybe," Manjit says, voice high with hope, head dancing Dogger-like with possibilities, "you're the heir to a fortune, like millions of pounds, like on telly."

Birdy lets herself count how many lofts she could build with that, before knocking them down, *crack-smack*. "I doubt it," she replies. "Or we wouldn't be living on Beasley Street, would we?"

"I s'pose not." Manjit nods at the truth of it. "So this Will Fitzsimmons bloke. Who's he?"

"He's from Leeds University," Birdy says, like it's a foreign land, not just over the way. "My mam met him there."

"So he's clever, then," Manjit decides.

"Aye." And Birdy feels pride swell her chest at the thought of him, of her own dad with all them books and words.

"Probably rich by now." Manjit's still spinning his story. "Probably running a conglomerate or summat, in't he?"

"I don't know," Birdy admits.

Manjit stops dead so Birdy has to take a step back to stand beside him.

"You mean you've not Googled him?" he says, like she's stupid.

Maybe she is stupid now she thinks about it. Because what did she reckon she were going to do? Knock on every door from here to Halifax 'til he opened one and said, "Birdy, my Birdy, you've found me"?

She shrugs, hoping her face in't as red as her gob.

But Manjit don't care, don't even shake his head or call her daft, just says, "Come on, then," and starts hurrying up the road so fast she has to scurry after, lest she loses him.

"Come where?" she calls. "I thought we were going to do the birds."

"Birds can wait," he calls back. "And you'll see."

She already knew which house was Manjit's, had seen it when she were going round Grandpa's, seen him and his sisters mucking about the front with balls and bicycles and a radio Sadie said were too loud when they walked past one day, though Grandpa don't mind. But she'd never been in before, never dared knock on the red door. She watches now as Manjit sticks his hand down his shirt, pulls out a key on a string, slots it into the lock, turns and pushes, the hallway opening up before him like a path.

"You coming, then?" he calls back to her.

"Aye," she replies. And she follows him down the path as if it were yellow brick, not red, and it were Oz itself at the end.

It's not Oz, but it's not 27 Beasley Street, neither. That house – her house – smells of perm lotion and shop-bought shepherd's pie. This one is so rich with scent it's a wonder it don't leak out steam: incense and spice and spray-on deodorant all fighting to be noticed. It's the same on the walls and all: photographs, hundreds of them all clamouring for attention. There's old men in hats and women in gold; there's babies, loads of them, some of them Manjit, small as a doll; and there's Manjit's dad, a proud, smiling, swollen version of the son on his knee, like someone's just taken a bicycle pump and inflated him.

"You want a Coke or owt?"

Birdy comes to. "No," she says. "You're all right." She's itching to get started, truth be told, can feel it inside her, a sort of electricity that crackles sharp as the photo itself.

Manjit gets himself one, though, snaps it open so she can hear the fizz that matches her own, then heads upstairs. "Come on, then," he calls down, and for the second time that afternoon, she does what she's asked and follows.

"Here."

The stool don't look big enough for two, only a few inches of faded velvet left once he's sat, but the armchair's too big and heavy to lug and besides, it's trapped the other side of the bed, so it's this or nowt. And Dogger in't around to see her, she s'poses, so he can't say owt.

"I've not got nits," Manjit says. "If that's what you're worried about."

"It's not," she replies as she squeezes herself in beside him.

"Not that you could catch 'em now," he adds.

Birdy can feel a smile dance on her lips, lets it out in a burst of laughter. "'Least Casey can't call me fleabag any more," she says.

"Nits only like clean hair, anyway," says Manjit, handing over another fact with his grin. "So she's the fleabag. In fact, I bet even her fleas have got fleas."

Birdy gives him a grin back. "So what shall we Google?" she asks.

"How about . . ." Manjit starts typing, *clickety-clack*, *clickety-clack*, on the finger-dirty keys. " . . . this."

Birdy watches as a name takes shape.

W–i–l–l–i–a–m

F–i–t–z–s–i–m–m–o–n–s

"Go on, then."

"Go on what?" Birdy asks.

"Press 'Enter'," he says. "That's the best bit and it's your search so you should do it."

"Right." Birdy touches her right forefinger, sweaty with want, on the key, holds her breath again as she pushes down, a big suck in as she waits for the truth to be revealed.

But this truth is a deflated balloon and she lets out its slow sigh as a hundred possibilities fill the screen: an eleven-year-old William who thinks he's in Slytherin; a black solicitor William who lives in Belfast; a guitarist in New Zealand, famous, and with freckles like her own so Birdy has high hopes for him until she sees he's only twenty-four.

"That's okay," Manjit says, half to himself. "We just need to narrow it down."

"How?" Birdy asks.

"Well, what else do you know about him?"

Birdy thinks. "He went to Leeds University?" she says.

"And how old is he?"

"How the heck should I know?"

"Well, how old's your mam? I mean, sorry, how old would your mam have been?"

Birdy's not got time for tears, not the sort either, just does the maths double quick. "Thirty-two."

"So we can guess he's about the same. I mean they look about the same, don't they?"

Birdy pulls the photo out her pocket where it's been since lunch – safer there, she thought – smooths it down on the desk where they can both see.

"He looks maybe a bit older," she says.

Manjit shakes his head. "I reckon that's the beard," he says. "Deceptive things, beards."

"Aye," agrees Birdy, as if she knows. She should know, what with Sadie being a hairdresser and all, and always banging on about braiding and beards, but when Sadie starts talking it's like a switch shuts off in Birdy's head and all she can hear is *squawk-squawk-squawk.*

"Wait, I've got it."

119

On the end of the name, Manjit types "Leeds University, English literature" and a year. Not the year Will Fitzsimmons might have been born, but the year Birdy were born.

"What's that?"

"The year he and your mam left university. You said she had you that summer, didn't you?"

"Aye?"

"So that's graduation year. That'll come up. Has to."

"Blimey!" Birdy's amazed at this boy. She thought Dogger were clever, cleverer than her, but he don't have the internet – in't allowed, 'cause his mam says TV and computers make your eyes go square and your brain turn to purple jelly – and this is almost magic.

Please let it be magic.

She presses "Enter" again and – open sesame, *abracadabra!* – this time there's no guitarists and no barely-men and no solicitors. There's an article from a few years back, from a newspaper, and a photo besides. No beard in this one, and no cake, but the same crinkled-corner eyes caught by the camera, the same smile. **William "Fitz" Fitzsimmons**, it says. **Scotland's youngest head teacher takes on Portobello Primary.**

"Portobello." Birdy says the word out loud, smooth and round and solid, another pebble of truth.

This is him. They've found him. They've found her dad.

Manjit's fingers fly now.

"What are you doing?" Birdy asks.

"Finding the school. It'll have a phone number."

Birdy feels a quickening in her chest. "Then what?"

"Then you call him."

"I can't. I mean, I don't want to – to call," she says, her words so fast they fall over each other. "What if I get the secretary?" She's thinking of Mrs Leech, whose beady eyes catch children who are late or lurking or lying about why they've not brought their lunch money.

But Manjit's not stopping. "So email," he says.

"I don't have an address."

"We'll get you one."

"I—"

Birdy don't get to finish that thought, let alone sentence, because Manjit's done it, stuck in his thumb and pulled out a plum. Fitz's personal email. Straight to him. No secretary stood wide and in the way.

Next he's on Google, setting up an email account for her and all.

"What's your mam's name again?"

"Bonnie," she says. "Bonnie Henderson. Why?"

"'Cause he probably gets hundreds of emails every day. Spam and others selling stuff, so he's not going to notice anything from a Jones, even if it's got Birdy in front of it. He might not even know that's your name. But your mam's name – he'll know that, won't he?"

Birdy can't argue with that logic, it's A+ gold-star stuff. But it don't feel right, sits odd on her and she says so. "It'd be lying, though, wouldn't it? Pretending to be someone else. You're not ... no one's supposed to do that on the internet. Miss Higgins said."

"Okay, so we just use Henderson, that's not lying. That were your name, weren't it?"

Birdy nods, remembering the plushness of it. "And 'B'," she says then.

"Be what?"

"No, the letter 'B'," she says, glad of getting one over Manjit for once. "It were her initial and it's mine so that's not lying, neither."

"Brilliant," Manjit agrees.

"And you could put 'Leeds' in it and all," she says, on a roll now, Sherlock and Moriarty all in one. "Like 'B-Henderson-Leeds'. Or something," she adds, in case she's got it wrong.

But she hasn't. Manjit thinks it's a cracker of an idea and types it in and then – hey presto! – that's her address.

"Now we've to write something," Manjit

says. "Well, you've to." And he shuffles the stool along so she's sat proper, square on the screen and keyboard.

"What shall I say?" Birdy asks, her voice no more than a fledgling pirrip now.

"You know what to say," Manjit pirrips in reply. And Birdy finds she does, has known it all along.

Dear Will Fitzsimmons,

   I don't know if you'll know who I am but I know you. I've a photo of you at Leeds University (see attached scan) in the summer before you left. I'd really like to talk to you about something important so could you please email me back on this address?

   Yours sincerely,

   B Henderson

P.S. If this isn't the right Will, then I'm sorry for bothering you, but could you please also email me back to let me know?

P.P.S. Either way, congratulations on being the youngest head teacher in Scotland. The head at our primary (Mr Newton) is fifty-seven and looks like Gandalf.

Then she waves the magic wand and presses "Send". "Now what?" she asks, a drum roll building in her head and heart.

"Now," Manjit says. "Now, we clean out the birds. And we wait."

Chapter Eight

Birdy can't wait, though, not for long. Soon as she's through the front door, she's off to the computer, tiger-fast and just as stealthy, sneaking into the study while Sadie's up to her elbows in shampoo. She knows the password, it's written in big letters and Sellotaped inside the desk drawer, so's Sadie don't forget and Dad knows how to spell it. Birdy told 'em they weren't to do that, that it were a "security risk", but no one listened, like usual, too busy with swimming and hair and life. Now she's glad of it, though, glad she's no more than a shadow slipping through cracks, so she can clickety-clack and log herself on to the computer without even having to ask.

Manjit's given her the name and password for the email and she's in there swift, scanning the inbox for something, anything. But all that's arrived is Manjit's "testing, testing" and a "Welcome B-Henderson-Leeds" from the email team. Birdy imagines them then, that team: pinging emails here and there across miles and mountains. "Do mine," she urges them, and clicks "Refresh" with everything invisibly crossed, but there's nowt more, not even spam.

She checks again after dinner, when Sadie's got Minnie in the bath, and again when Dad's busy telling her the story of *The Three Little Pigs* and huffing and puffing so hard Birdy thinks he might well blow this house down. But the walls stay solid, not even a shiver and the big bad wolf gives up. Only what Birdy don't remember when she's tip-tip-tapping and hoping is that wolves have all sorts of other business: eating Grandma, dressing up in sheep's clothing, and keeping a beady eye on Birdy and all.

She's thought of something else to search for. 'Cause she's tired of everyone slipping through her fingers like they're nowt but fog, tired of not having facts. So she types it in, just one word: Dogger.

But all that comes up is pictures of a little kids' book about a boy and a lost toy, and that the word's an old boat, two-masted and bluff-bowed and used for fishing. Nowt about her friend at all. It would help if she knew the rest of his name, or where he lived; it would help if he told her the truth, not the tales he makes up for her amusement. Sometimes she's wondered if he's even real, so mist-thin is he, so insubstantial. But Grandpa knows his name, don't he? And Dad too, though he don't like to say so. Maybe she should tell Manjit and all, maybe . . .

"What do you think you're up to?"

Birdy starts at Sadie's voice and her stomach

jumps. "Nowt," she says quick, and clicks off the page so the photo of Dad and Sadie in a shower of confetti fills the screen, but it's too late.

"D'you think you get computer time after what you've done to yer 'ead?" Sadie says.

Birdy don't know what to say because the answer's yes but she knows that's not what Sadie wants to hear. "I . . . " she begins and then tries a "sorry?" in case that's the magic word.

It's not.

"Love, you're barred off that for a week. I thought your dad'd told you."

Birdy shakes her head. "What if . . . " She clutches at something, hopes it's the key. "What if I've got homework?"

It's not.

"You'll have to do it at school," says Sadie. "Or wait until your dad or me can do it with you."

Like that'd ever happen. "But—" she protests.

"But nowt. You're lucky you're not barred from the birds and all." Sadie sticks her hands on her hips. "It's your grandpa you've got to thank for that."

"For being ill?"

"Don't be smart with me, young lady."

Birdy don't understand. "I'm not, I—"

"That's enough. Go on, get to bed. You can read, or write in that booklet of yours."

Birdy don't say owt else, just tramps upstairs, though the thoughts in her head are ten a penny, tripping over themselves to find space. Maybe she will write in that booklet, once she knows who her dad is. Once she knows who *she* is. 'Cause even if she don't know that, there's one thing she understands now, and that's that she don't fit here, not with Sadie, and not with the man pretending to be her dad, neither. It's not Minnie's fault, Birdy don't mind her, not really, but the grown-ups, they should know better. And one day, soon, they will.

On Tuesday she meets Manjit at the gate and he tells her he's checked her email account this morning and there's nowt, not from William Fitzsimmons.

"But at least it's not bounced back," he says, looking on the bright side, always on the bright side, "Or worse, said, 'no, it's not me, wrong man,' or summat."

"Aye," says Birdy, though she can't see the light so clearly through the gloom as him.

On Wednesday there's nowt again.

On Thursday there's still not a dicky bird but Manjit's got something for her, anyway.

"What's that?" she asks, though she can see for herself it's a mobile phone, and a good one and all.

"It's our Samira's," he tells her. "Well, was. Only she's upgraded and I'm s'posed to get it, but I don't mind my old phone for a bit longer, so I thought you could have it, just 'til you get one of your own."

"That'll be never," Birdy says. "Sadie says we can't afford one."

"Well, you can have this one now," Manjit tells

her. "It's got some credit left on it. Nearly eight pounds fifty. And I've put email on it, see?"

Birdy sees. Sees the same account he's set up for her, sees the inbox with the two emails sat skulking, waiting for a third to slink in and sit on top, sees the glimmering bright, just the same as him, and grins. "Thank you," she says, feeling it cold and solid in her hand. Feelings its heft, its importance.

"Now you can check whenever you want. Long as you don't use up the credit. And as long as you keep it safe and secret."

"I will," Birdy promises. Same as she's kept Manjit's number safe and secret and all, not knowing what to do with it, where to put it. Until now.

She texts him that night: Coming for the toss tomorrow?

Def, he texts back. Then: That means definitely in case you were wondering? Which she was.

So, still with no word but from each other, on

Friday they set to scraping off the perches while they wait for Grandpa to finish watching the horse racing and start up the van.

That's when she tells him.

"I've another friend," she says to Manjit. No more than that at first. She's testing the water, see, finding out if the fact sinks or swims.

"Oh, aye," he says. "What's her name?"

"It's a he," she corrects him. Then takes a big breath, enough to carry his name out so heavy it weighs. "Dogger," she tells him. Then again, "His name's Dogger."

"Funny old name," says Manjit. "He's not at our school, then."

Birdy shakes her head. "He's not at any school. His mam teaches him at home. When she's not ill," she adds.

"Lucky," Manjit says. "Imagine that. No maths and no lumpy custard and no Casey Braithwaite going on and on."

"Aye." Birdy lets out a laugh.

Manjit drops a spade of mess into the pail. "So where is he, then?"

Birdy shrugs. "No idea," she says and it's not a lie. She's not seen him proper, to talk to, since he shaved her head. "I think his mam might be sick again," she says, plucking a possibility from thin air and turning it into truth.

"Can I meet him?" Manjit says.

Birdy says nowt to that, 'cause she knows what Dogger'd say, knows he don't want to meet Manjit, though why she don't rightly know because Manjit's all right. More than all right. Look at the things he does for her, not even waiting to be asked. Look at him now, bird poo on his hands and in his hair, not even caring. "Thanks," she says.

Manjit looks up from Marilyn. "For what?"

Birdy shrugs. "Stuff."

Manjit nods. "You're all right."

They work in silence for a bit, enjoying the thrum of the birds, each other's company without having to say owt. That's when they hear it, the pirrip of a new one, a fledgling fresh from the egg, only a day in the world, if that. Then, eyes agog at each other, both guessing what's up, they tiptoe, soft like the tigers, only toothless this time, to see.

"It's one of Queenie's," Manjit whispers. "Best breeder, your grandpa reckons."

"Aye," Birdy agrees. "Billy Bremner's one of hers, and Marilyn."

"And half the flock, truth be told," says Grandpa, soft on his feet as an old lion himself. But Birdy and Manjit can't take their eyes off the baby, it's too-wide mouth and too-thin skin.

"Ugly little thing it is now," Grandpa says, seeing what they're thinking. "But it'll be right soon, mark my words. As beautiful as Billy and just as fast, at least if we keep it fed and our fingers crossed."

"What's it called?" Manjit asks.

And that's when Birdy turns to catch Grandpa's wink, nods her reply back, 'cause she can't do one eye that well, only blink and that's not the same. "You pick," she says, heart full like she's handing her friend the gift of life itself.

"Me?" Manjit asks.

"Aye," Grandpa says. "You've helped out and I can't pay you, so think of it like a reward. And make it a good one," he adds. "'Cause it'll be the last. Any more and Harry'll have to think 'em up."

Birdy tries not to think about Harry having the pigeons and what that means ... She tries names for size herself in her head, ones he's plucked from other people's stories: Dorothy and Glinda and Mr Tumnus.

But Manjit's got other ideas, other names, one in particular. "Fitz," he says.

Birdy shuffles, not sure what he's up to. "What if it's not a boy?" she says quick, looking at Grandpa for a get-out clause.

Grandpa shrugs. "Who says Fitz is a boy's name?" he asks. "No rule there. And I think it's grand-sounding. Like royalty. Like a princess."

"Or a prince," adds Manjit.

"Aye," says Grandpa. "That too. A handsome one."

Come to rescue me, Birdy thinks, *a knight in shining armour.* She looks at the bird, scrawny and small. It don't look very prince-like. 'Least not yet. But then nor does that man in the photograph and he might still turn out to be one, and she touches the phone that sits snug in her pocket to be sure it's there.

"Come on, then," Grandpa says. "Time for the toss."

"Can we take Fitz?" Manjit asks. "Not for flying, just for the fun."

"Don't be daft," Birdy says. "He'll not be allowed out for weeks yet."

Manjit shrugs, says some soft words to the bird he already sees as his, and goes with his friend to start the loading. Then the pair of them, heads full of handsome princes, head up Cop Hill in the creaking, coughing van with creaking, coughing

Grandpa and a crate full of birds to let fly, and all their hopes with them.

What Birdy don't know yet, though, is that hope's a dangerous thing. When hope's all you've got, chances are you're done for.

She's about to find out.

Chapter Nine

"Where is he?" asks Birdy.

She's hopping, foot to foot in the back garden, Manjit beside her, hands like binoculars over his eyes, Grandpa still in the loft checking he's not missed owt, missed him 'cause he's so quick he's been back half an hour and's asleep in someone else's bed.

But he's not. There's no sign of him in or out.

Billy Bremner's lost.

"He'll be right," Grandpa says. "He'll just be busy, stopped off for some bother with another bird, I'll warrant."

"Does he do that a lot?" Manjit asks, already doubtful.

"No," admits Grandpa. "But there's always a first time."

Birdy don't think it's bother with birds, though, don't even think he's lost. He's just had enough, knows what's coming, that he's moving to Harry's and there's nowt anyone can do to stop it. Unless ... she runs into the shed, checks her phone quick, the light blue in the gloom. But there's still nowt new, so she clicks it off, careful not to waste the battery.

"Go on home," Grandpa says eventually. "I'll ring your dad soon as there's sight of him."

"What about me?" asks Manjit. "Will you ring me?"

Grandpa laughs, a gurgly sound that turns to a cough. "Tell you what," he says, when he can push the words out. "I'll knock for you, tell you what's what."

But he don't call and he don't knock and next

morning, when Birdy skips breakfast to check the loft, there's still no sign of Billy.

She sits on the bench next to Grandpa, who's there with his *Racing News* and his tea and his pipe. Been there a while, by the look of that brew, half-drunk and cold, the kettle scum drifting on the surface like dirt.

"Have you asked around?" Birdy says.

"Aye," Grandpa replies. "Word's out to the whole club to call if they catch him."

"What if . . . ?" Birdy starts. But she don't finish it, not in her head or out loud. She's still clinging on to hope, see. Got to. For now.

"Like I said, he'll be all right," Grandpa says, and he takes another swig of his cold, cloudy cuppa.

They sit like that, quiet in the morning sunlight, until the phone tring-trings back in the house and, while Birdy's heart pitter-patters, Grandpa clatters in to get it, then out again, quicker than Birdy's seen him move in a while.

"Is it Billy?" she asks, breathless with want. "Is he landed?"

But Grandpa shakes his head. "Not Billy," he says. "Sadie. You were supposed to be somewhere half an hour ago."

Birdy tries to remember, searches in the swirl of the things Sadie's told her, the "do"s and the "don't"s and the "will you"s and "stoppit"s and "be back by"s. And there it is, emerging from the blur: "Be back by ten, 'cause we're going to see the new house."

In her head she thinks a Dogger swear. "Oh, blimey," she says out loud.

"Blimey indeed," says Grandpa. "Now go on, get. I'll be fine waiting here."

Birdy don't feel convinced. Don't look it, neither.

"If I need company I'll find Manjit," Grandpa says. "Or Dogger, even."

Birdy nods then. "Dogger," she says. "You should find him." 'Cause he's lost and all, has been for a week now.

"I will," Grandpa says. "Only if I need to, though. Now shoo."

So Birdy shoos, knowing she'll only be in more trouble the longer she stays.

"What'd you think you were up to?" Dad demands as she clatters in the door.

"I . . ." But she knows he knows, so what's the point?

"Answer your dad," Sadie adds. Then changes her mind. "No, don't bother, we're already late as it is." She reaches to brush something off Birdy, mud or worse. "Blimey, when did you last wash?"

Birdy shrugs. Not like showers have been top of her list.

"Well, there's no time now," Sadie says, face still sour as gone-off milk. "You'll just have to make do. But at least change your top. And use some deodorant and all."

"I en't got any," Birdy says, face hot with shame. Not like she don't know she needs it. But she can't ask her dad, not that he'd notice, and as for Sadie . . .

"You . . . Use mine," Sadie says then.

Birdy looks to see if it's a trick or a lie. But Sadie's not smiling.

"On the windowsill in the bathroom. Be quick, mind."

Birdy's quick, pulls off her top, slip-slops the stuff under her arms, then stands sentinel, arms out as she waits for it to dry. She listens through the grate, hearing them slating her, despairing. "It's one thing after another," she hears from Sadie. "She thinks of no one but herself." "She does too," argues Minnie. "She thinks about the birds." That only proves Sadie's point. "Exactly," she says. Birdy waits for her dad to defend her, to say she's got a lot on her plate, with school, and with Billy Bremner missing – the bits he knows about. But he's shut his gob, or Sadie's shut it for him long ago because there's nowt but silence, then Sadie again, "Will you hurry up, love!" and that's to her, not the others, so, sticky-pitted, she grabs a clean T-shirt, a zoo one from last summer, and comes downstairs, better-smelling but still, unmistakably, Birdy.

"You don't want to wear a hat?" Sadie asks as they climb into the cab. "Only your nana's coming."

She's not my nana, thinks Birdy. Never has been and glad of it, she is, with her mithering and moaning, same as Sadie. But she says nowt.

"Does she like hats?" Minnie asks. "Can I wear a hat?"

"No." Sadie sighs, teeth gritted.

"So why does Birdy need one?"

Birdy feels it bubble out, borne on the wings of a lost bird and still-to-be-found father. "'Cause I look weird."

"No," insists Sadie, surprising Birdy.

"No," her dad echoes, finally finding his voice.

"She does too," says Minnie, lies too complicated for her yet, even white ones. "You do," she says, turning to Birdy next to her.

145

"So what?" Birdy says back. "What's it to you?"

"Mam," wails Minnie. "Birdy bossied me."

"She started it," Birdy says, 'cause she's not taking the blame this time.

Sadie heaves her bulk round, leans through the gap between the seats. "Will you stop it, the pair of you," she says. "This is supposed to be nice. We're supposed to be having a family day out. So act like one, can't you?"

Birdy imagines Manjit's family, squeezing into their seven-seater, all laughing and smiling and sucking on lollipops. Or Dogger's, even, him and his mam, tight as you like, never fighting, just exploring the world together through books and stories she tells him as he sits on her lap, or snuggled on the sagging orange beanbag he's told her about.

Then she pictures Fitz, her and him doing the same, lolling on a sofa – leather, or tartan, maybe – in Portobello. It's by the sea, she knows that now, in the middle of a city but still with sand and waves and ice cream in the summer. And on the top of the hill a castle looking down over them. Maybe he lives there, prince that he might be. Maybe—

"Seat belt!" she hears suddenly. "How many times?"

And she's back in the cab with the fake dad, the pretender. And silent, sombre, Birdy buckles up for the ride across town to another house, and another life she's already decided isn't ever going to be hers.

Sadie's mam don't like the hair, says it's "different" in a voice that means "weird", but she does like the house, high up on the hill. Can't stop sing-songing its praises as they walk around the three bedrooms and through-lounge. "Look at that, Sadie, look at that sink, it's got built-in waste disposal."

"It had better, for what we're paying for it," Dad mutters. "It had better do its own ironing for that."

"Like you do any ironing," says Sadie, laughing, and her and Nana Hooton give each other a look that says "men" and has a heavy sigh built into it and all.

"Don't need to," says Dad. "Nature's own iron, me. All that body heat." And he grabs Sadie and gives her a kiss and then it's her and Dad giving each other looks and Nana rolling her eyes.

Birdy's had enough, takes herself off to the forty-foot garden with crazy paving and ornamental water feature. Dad says he's paving that over soon as and all, crazy or otherwise. "Drowning risk," he says. Minnie insists she won't have an accident, that she can swim in it, even, but Dad's having none of it. Birdy don't blame him. It's a horrible thing. Green with muck and a fish floating bloated on the surface, dead-eyed as a toy.

She sits herself – *plop* – on a plastic chair, looks down the garden at the city beyond, at her side of town, hers and Grandpa's and Manjit's. She can see the transmitter over on Cop Hill, see the route

Billy should've flown back. There's birds here now, tweeting their stories and conversations to each other, sparrows and finches and pigeons. But none of them's Billy and she's itching to get back.

"Come see this, Birdy!" she hears Dad call from above her, and looks up at a window to see him hanging out, beckoning her with his big hand. "This'll be yours," he says. "Come on."

But Birdy don't want to see, no point, and turns back to her watching and waiting.

"Suit yourself," says Dad.

And she does.

She suits herself through her ham and pineapple pizza, not saying owt, just chewing slowly, the bread clagging in her mouth so's she can hardly swallow. Through the glass of cola at Nana's, not even real Coke, flat and funny-tasting so she wants to spit it back out, but only Dogger'd be that daring. Through the car ride home, where Minnie's telling everyone all the things of wonder the house has got – a fridge with a tap for water in the door, lights that can dim, a blue toilet – like she's reeling off her list to Santa. But Birdy don't care what it's got, all she cares about is: first, finding Billy Bremner; second, finding Fitz; and third, finding Dogger, and soon as they pull up outside the house, she's out the car door and off down the road to Grandpa's, to see what's what at the loft.

He's still sat there with his pipe and paper, a bottle of ale now instead of tea. But there's no Manjit, no Dogger and, worse, no Billy Bremner.

"He'll come back," Grandpa insists. "They always do. Only fly one way, don't they?"

He waits for Birdy to nod a yes. But she's silent still, so he has to prod her again.

"And what way's that?"

"Home," she whispers eventually.

But it's not home, is it. Not for long. She knows that and maybe so does Billy. Maybe even Dogger, that's why he's not bothered coming back. It's just Grandpa who's not facing up to it.

"Your Manjit came over earlier," Grandpa says then.

"He's not *my* Manjit," she says. Though maybe he is, a little bit. Or the birds', anyway. "Was he looking for Billy?"

"Aye, lass. Billy." Grandpa swallows a swig of beer. "And you."

"What'd he want me for?"

"Says you're to check something, and call him. Homework, maybe."

Birdy feels another seed of hope sow inside her, tries to wheedle it out the soil before it takes root, 'cause she's learning now not to let it grow too much, knows how much that hurts when it's cut down. "Aye," she says. "It'll be homework. I'd . . . I'd best be off."

Grandpa smiles, seeing nothing, and everything. "You'd best had, hadn't you."

And she skitters up the path, a barely-able baby bird, unsteady on her feet, bashing into bushes and crashing into the gate post before she's out on the pavement and her hand's in her pocket and switching on her phone.

She waits.

And waits.

And waits.

And this time it comes, drops into her inbox with that delicious ding:

From: W.Fitzsimmons@portobello.ac.uk

Birdy hovers her finger over it, heart drumming, then, deep breath, a tap, and — *abracadabra!* — she's in.

Dear Bonnie, it begins.

I can't believe it's you.

Chapter Ten

It were his fault – Fitz's. She weren't going to pretend to be someone else, make out she were her mam, but he assumed it and so she were just going along with his mistake. Not like real lying, not really.

That's what she tells herself, anyway, as she tip-taps out her reply, all fat thumbs and spelling mistakes and having to start three times before it even makes any sense.

Dear Fitz, she writes back. Yes, it's me. She answers all his questions – where she's living now (In Leeds still. I never really left); isn't it funny that they've both ended up teaching (I know, fancy that!); does she have her eyes on Mr Newton's job (Maybe one day, only I really like Year Six, except for Casey Braithwaite who's a head bigger than Cop Hill and a gob on her like the gutter); is she married (No way); and how's motherhood, how many's she got now? (It's grand. I've just got the one – Bridie – who's inherited a liking for books, but has also surprised everyone with her talent in pigeon racing. So I don't want any more because they'd never turn out as good as her, not in a million years.)

She weren't going to put the last bit, deleted it, 'cause it sounded swollen-headed, something Casey might say. Only then she thinks that actually that's something a mam would put, a real one, the sort of thing Manjit's or Dogger's mam would say, the sort of thing Sadie's always saying about Minnie, so she taps it out again, signs off: love Bonnie and presses "Send" before she can change her mind.

She's asked him stuff and all. Is he married? Has

he got a girlfriend? Does he have kids? She's got her fingers crossed for "no"s, don't want another stepmum and step-brothers and sisters getting in the way, or taking up his time, the time he'll have for her. 'Course, she's not got to that bit yet, scared to ask or say it outright. Instead she's hoping he'll get the clue – about the brain for maths and English – that he'll say, "But you were no good at sums, that were me," and then he'll guess and it'll all be done up quick and neat like a tidy parcel and he'll ask her up to Edinburgh on the next train.

Wouldn't that be a bobby dazzler?

Manjit reckons so. He's made up for her, he says, saw the email come in yesterday and was bursting to tell her but he daren't call her house, 'case Sadie heard. He tells her she should keep her mobile switched on at all times.

"I can't," Birdy tells him. "'Cause of the battery."

"Oh!" Manjit slaps a hand to his forehead. "I should've given you a charger. I'll bring it tomorrow. Or you could come round after school for it?"

In the end she does that, pops in for a charger and a Coke and a go of his PlayStation before they do the birds. 'Cause she loves it here, in this family-filled house with everyone chitter-chattering, happy to be cramped in together like the birds. But this time they're both nervous, him spilling drink on his shoes and her dropping the controller three times. It's Billy, see, he's in their heads and they're desperate to get round there to see if he's back, and desperate to stay here 'case he's not. But the clock creeps round to five and Birdy knows she's not got long, 'cause Sadie says she's to be back by six latest 'cause it's spag bol for tea. Birdy don't know why she's bothered cooking her favourite, thinks it's a trick, like the deodorant she found on her bed yesterday. But she's trying to be good, no point kicking off if she's going away soon, anyway, don't want to raise suspicions. 'Cause what if they find out and lock her up, after all?

"Come on," Birdy says. "We better get going."

"Aye," Manjit agrees. "Poo won't clear itself."

And that's all they say, all they *can* say; it's in silence they walk the four doors down, in silence they check the perches for Billy, but still no sign. It's only then that Birdy digs deep enough to find words.

"He'll come back," she says, as they check on Fitz, make sure the baby bird is safe and warm and watered, at least. "They only fly one way, so he's got to."

She says it for Manjit, she tells herself, and for Grandpa, who's shut in the house, his lungs are bad today, too bad to even come to the loft. But it's for her and all.

"Do you really think so?" Manjit asks. "Or are you just saying that?"

Birdy looks at him, into his brown eyes, conker-bright and wide with want. "A bit of both," she says, and it's the first totally true thing she's said in a while.

*

She checks her phone again soon as she's back home in her bedroom, door shut and leaning against it.

That night, as she lies in bed, with the phone charging underneath – hidden in an old shoebox of her own she's started, along with a four-leaf clover Manjit found up Cop Hill, a pair of dice she dug up from the garden one summer, and that photo – nine times, she checks, each time promising this'll be the last and then she'll go to sleep for sure, but each time there's nowt back from Fitz. He'll be busy, she tells herself. Marking homework and . . . and whatever business it is head teachers do.

It's the same on Tuesday, and Wednesday too. No Billy Bremner, no Dogger and no Fitz – no man-Fitz, anyway, the baby bird is doing just fine, fattening up and feathering out. Manjit's been talking to him, telling him how to grow and fly, telling him what's what so he's ready in a few weeks for take-off.

Grandpa knows it's just bird sense and Queenie that's doing it, but he says nowt and nor does Birdy because it's good to have some happiness in the loft. She touches her pocket then, a habit now – a good-luck touch – willing it to bring her a message, to ping it through the air on wide wings, 'cause that's how she imagines it, like the notes she sends Grandpa to tell him what's for tea. Not that he ever shows up for it.

But it don't make a sound, not even a buzz, like the tremble of a fledgling. It sits sullen and silent all the way home, and all through tea and all through her shower that Sadie's told her she's to have at least three times a week now.

"Come on, Fitz," she says as she slips the phone into the shoebox, says her good night to it and all the other precious things she's got stored, picks up *The Silver Sword* from beside her bed and opens where she left off last night. "Talk to me. Tell me summat, anything."

And at two minutes past midnight – Birdy's

nose still buried in the book; the world outside reduced to stragglers and shift workers, foxes and owls; the rest of the house in soft, snoring slumber – he does.

My Bonnie,

   I still can't believe I'm talking to you. Or, truthfully, (because it's late and I'm two whiskys to the wind) I can't believe we ever lost touch. But things happen. Life happens, I suppose, and you did living so well. And you had Bridie, anyway (what a name – I love it). I'm glad she's thriving.

At her name – her real name – Birdy feels her wings unfurl, the promise of him calling to her, pulling her home. She reads on.

And no, I'm not married. I was, once, briefly. To a girl called Nerys Edwards from teacher training, who could touch her nose with the tip of her tongue and was allergic to peas, though neither of these contributed to our downfall.

God, Bonnie, I have so many questions for you! Things I don't want to ask on here. Do you have a number I can call? Or would that be too weird? Maybe. It's just that I'd love to hear your voice again. You can sing to me – Bob Marley or Van.

Actually, that would definitely be weird. Too strange to go back to that summer.

But I would really like to talk.

Love, always, Fitz x

Dogger thinks he sounds like an eejit.

He shows up at last, can't stay away when there's news this big. He's waiting in the loft for her Thursday when Manjit's had to go to the dentist's for a filling. It's like he knows, like he's been avoiding him. Though she can't think why when Manjit's as kind as you like.

161

"I thought he'd be more grown up," he says. "Use longer words. Or Scottish ones. He don't sound like a rock star."

"'Cause he's not," Birdy tells him. "He's a teacher, I told you."

"Sounds boring to me."

"Manjit don't think so."

"Manjit sounds boring and all. Playing on gadgets all the time. Gadgets are for eejits."

"Whatever." Birdy pushes the phone back in her pocket, puffed up with crossness. She'd thought he'd be pleased for her, want to celebrate or summat, but instead he's just spat on the cinders and put the fire out.

They sit at odds for a second, him cross-legged on the chair, elbows on his knees, her cross-armed against the wooden wall, like stalemate, neither of them wanting to budge, like her and Minnie when they've argued over the telly and Sadie says neither of them can watch owt they're being so daft. Then it's always her who gives in, 'cause she's the oldest and Dad – that man – says that's how it works.

This time it's him, though – Dogger. Not 'cause he's the oldest – though he is, he reckons, though only by hours, 'cause their birthdays are exactly the same – but because he's bigger, and braver, and full-hearted, whatever Dad reckons.

"So d'you think you'll call him?" he asks.

Birdy shakes her head. "How can I?" she asks, still bristling a bit but trying not to. "I don't sound like a grown-up teacher, do I?"

"Not really," Dogger admits.

"I just told him I'd lost my phone but to keep emailing."

Dogger nods, she's done good.

"How's your mam?" Birdy asks, glad they're back to best friends, Manjit forgotten, for now, though Birdy flinches when she thinks of the drill.

"She's singing," he says, his voice fat with satisfaction. "So today's a good one, I reckon."

"That's grand," Birdy says and means it. Then

she remembers summat. "My mam sang," she says. "'Least Fitz said so. Bob Marley and someone called Van."

"I don't know them," says Dogger. "But we could do the bird song."

"Aye, all right," says Birdy.

And they do, they sing about the three little birds. Soft at first, so's not to disturb their own feathered friends, then louder, 'cause it's swelling in them, bursting to get out, all that hope and possibility and promise that it'll come good. In the end.

And that's when Grandpa walks in. And, behind him, Harry.

Harry's fat and fifty-nine with a limp and a bald head shinier than a new penny. "Like an egg," Grandpa says, when Harry's not about, which always makes Birdy laugh, but not today. There's nowt funny about him today.

"Copying me, I see." He nods at Birdy's own skull, down-covered now but still peeking though pinkly underneath.

"No," she says, moving back 'case he wants to touch it, like everyone seems to now, even Casey.

He don't try, just shrugs, like she's a mystery. "Right." He turns to Grandpa. "Let's 'ave 'em checked."

"What're you doing?" Birdy asks, following the men through the wire-netted door.

"Birdy," Grandpa warns.

But she don't heed it. "No, what's he up to? I want to know."

Grandpa gives Harry a look that says *be careful* but Harry's one for plain talk and telling it straight, always has been. "No point trying to polish a poo," he says and Birdy agrees; she wants to know what's going on. "I'm checking they're fit," he says.

"They are," says Birdy. "All of 'em."

"Well, if that's the case – and I'll be the judge of that, not you, mind – then I'll take 'em all, won't I? Save you scrabbling about for re-homing or wringing their necks."

Birdy's insides slip to her feet. "What?" she asks.

165

"He's having you on,' Grandpa says quick. "No one's wringing any necks."

"Not that," Birdy snaps, desperate. "Why's he taking any?"

"Birdy," Grandpa shakes his head. "Birdy, you know why."

Birdy does know why, but until someone says it, it's not real, she won't believe it.

"Next Monday, you said, Joe?" Harry asks, pushing Queenie to the side so's he can see Fitz, check the baby bird's as good as Grandpa reckons.

"Aye, Monday," Grandpa replies, a sigh of surrender.

"No," she says.

"Yes," Grandpa says.

"Not Fitz," Birdy pleads. "And not Marilyn, neither. You can't have her. She's mine!"

"And what're you going to do with her?" Grandpa asks, soft, his hands gently resting on her shoulders.

Birdy shakes 'em off like they're flies, but says nowt.

Dogger does, though. Spits out a swear, and then a second one.

"Hey," Grandpa scolds. "No need for that."

Birdy gives Dogger a look, gives Grandpa one and all.

But he ignores it. "And there's nowt you or I can do," he carries on. "So don't be trying owt, you hear me?"

Birdy nods, she does hear him.

But just because she hears him, don't mean there's nowt to be done.

There's always something. He's the one who taught her that: to never to give up, to always look for answers, for the bright side. She's not giving up on Billy coming back and she's not giving up on the other birds, neither. She'll beg if she has to, promise to eat her peas, to shower, to pick up her knickers, even pick up Minnie's knickers; whatever it takes to persuade Sadie and her dad to save the birds.

*

But Sadie's not buying it. "Birdy, love. You can't expect me or your dad to fetch you and your sister from school, then come back here and wait about for two hours while you faff about with pigeons."

"I like pigeons," says Minnie, dragging a fork through ketchup, drawing a fish.

"No, you don't," Sadie tells her.

"I could get the bus back after," Birdy offers. "It'd be fine."

"It'd be another two pound a day at least," says Sadie. "That's a tenner a week, for a start. And what about when you're at the new school?" She's on a roll now, lips gabbing, words jabbing at Birdy, 'least to her mind. "You can't be going there and back again on the bus by yourself every day and your dad can't drive you."

"It's his job," Birdy points out. "Why can't he?"

"Because you've not got the fare," Sadie says, her words getting shorter along with her temper. "He's got to be earning, not ferrying you about for free."

"But—" Birdy begins, her voice cracking to let a sob out.

"No buts," Sadie says, stamping on the sob sharpish. "I'm sorry, but we're moving house on Monday and that's that." She goes to the oven, yanks down the door and slams it up again. "And don't be mithering your dad with this, neither, he's got enough on his plate trying to find a van."

"Can I drive the van?" Minnie asks.

"Christ on a bike!" Sadie shouts then, so loud Minnie squawks and all, sorry for whatever she's said.

But Birdy knows it's not Minnie's fault, it's hers, Birdy's, it always is. She's the one that causes the bother, that makes her dad fret and Sadie swear so. And why? 'Cause she's not even theirs, is she. Neither of theirs.

She turns to trudge up the stairs, holding her breath to hold in the tears. She shouldn't be here.

A cuckoo, that's what she is, a cuckoo who's snuck into someone else's nest.

So she best be sneaking off out of it, hadn't she?

Dear Fitz,

You were right when you said we should talk. I could come to Edinburgh. Say, this Saturday? What's your address?

Please. I really need to see you.

Love, Bonnie x

P.S. I'll even do singing.

Chapter Eleven

Broughton Street. That's where Fitz is nested. He told her in an email, pinged her back straight away, saying she could come Saturday, stay as long as she liked, though he expects she's got to be back for school on Monday. Shame, that.

She can see it in her mind's eye: four floors tall with a room for each of them and a spare for when someone comes to stay. There's books from your feet to the ceiling and pictures too, of family – *her* family. Her real one, that is. There'll be a garden and all, not big mind, but big enough for a loft. Just a small one at first, so Marilyn can

settle. Then they'll get some land – an allotment
or summat – and get the birds back off Harry, the
whole flock. Retrain 'em so they know where to
fly back to. Not Leeds any more, but Scotland –
their new home.

'Course she's taking Marilyn. Got to, en't she?
'Cause Birdy's the one that trained her from when
she were no more than a fledgling like Fitz: that
fattened her up on seed and love; that let her out an
hour at a time to get used to the landing board; that
lifted the cage so she could spread her wings and
flap haphazard into the trees, then threw a tennis
ball to mither her down again. She's the one that
first tossed her up Cop Hill, then waited, breath
baited, for her to bob through the trap and peck
her seed like she'd only gone for stroll round the
corner, not flown her first five miles. So she'll be
the one to keep her now, whatever Grandpa says.

They're walking home from school when she
tells Manjit. He's not too keen. Not keen on any
of it, truth be told.

"It's not right," he tells her. "Running away. Sadie's not so bad. Or your dad."

"He's not my dad. And you started this," she tells him, indignant. "It were all your idea."

"Aye, to write to him," Manjit says. "But not to run. What'll Sadie say? What'll your grandpa say? And, besides, who's going to do the birds? 'Cause Harry's not coming for 'em 'til Monday, so someone's got to do food and cleaning 'til then. You didn't think of that, did you?"

He sounds like Sadie now, all fight and fluster and forcing himself in the way, right in Birdy's path. "I did and all think of that," she snaps back. "You can do 'em. You know what's what—"

"But—"

"And you can keep a look out for Billy Bremner," she adds quick. "And an eye on Fitz. He'll need you."

"Aye, I suppose," Manjit agrees, voice heavy with sulk.

But Birdy knows him and can see that his chest

is puffed and he's chuffed as anything to be asked. She's glad of it, but sad too, 'cause he loves them birds almost as much as her, almost as much as even Grandpa. Not that either of them'd let on. "Thanks," she says then.

"For what?" Manjit asks.

Birdy counts the ways: for helping find her real dad, for helping with the birds, for caring about them, for not caring what Casey Braithwaite thinks, for talking to her at all when everyone else inched away like she'd got the lurgy or the cheese touch . . .

"For the phone," she says. "And . . . and, you know."

"Aye," he replies. "You're all right." He rummages in his pocket, pulls out a packet of chews. "Here," he says.

"What's that for?" she asks.

"The journey," he says. "It's three hours and three minutes so you'll need summat."

Birdy takes them. "Ta," she says, and pushes

them into her pocket, though she don't reckon she'll eat them, barely been able to get her cereal down since she decided to go. "I'd best be off," she tells him. "Got to pack." She stops then, thinks of something. "You could come," she adds as they click-clack through the gate and along the gum-sticky pavement. "If you like. Not to stay, just to see me there and back."

But Manjit shakes his head. "Me mam'd have my guts for garters if I tried owt like that. Besides, the birds need me, you said so."

"Aye, I did," Birdy replies, though it's with a silent sigh. 'Cause if he were by her side she knows she'd be right, knows it would all turn out.

"I wish I could," he adds, and Birdy can see it's true, can see him grasping for the glimmering bright side, can see him picturing himself on a train to Scotland, wrapped in adventure like a sweet in silver tinfoil.

"I won't be on my own, though," she says to save him. "I mean, I'll have Marilyn."

"Aye, I s'pose."

"And I'll text you. Call, even. And you can call me, 'cause there'll be no one to say 'where the hell d'you get that phone, Birdy Jones?'"

Manjit laughs, so she can see the pale pink bubble gum wedged in the scarlet cavern of his mouth. "Aye," he says. "And I'll call you. Tell you what's what with the birds."

Birdy thinks. "And if Casey comes to school with her eyebrows drawn on again."

Manjit gets it. "Or if Dane Perry gets locked in the bogs."

"Or Flora Watts eats a worm for a dare."

"Or Riz Pickens is sick in his lunch."

"No, not that," Birdy says, face folded up like a pug.

"No, maybe not." Manjit's pushing his own gate back and forward now, back and forward, wafting air and wasting time. "See you."

He turns to go but then, without warning, turns back and wraps her in a hug. A tight, solid thing; a thing that smells of bubble gum and laughter; a thing so surprising it stiffens her at first, squeezing the very breath out of her so that she stands awkward, arms rigid at her sides, clutched by this boy, like a scared pigeon held by a too-eager child. But then something inside her softens, as if his smile has seeped from him into her, so that she finds her own arms snaking up and holding on to him tight too.

"Aye, see you," Birdy echoes, as he finally lets go.

Then, catching her breath back, she watches him walk – half skip, half swagger – watches him turn the key on a string and let himself into his house full of life, full of love. She touches her ribs with her fingers to feel where he hugged her, and to feel where her own key might hang, after tomorrow. Then turns and walks slowly back to Beasley Street for what she reckons is the last time. Last time she's going to see the rusting fridge sat in Nog Bates's garden, dead as the fox that sat outside number nine for a week. Last time she's going to nearly trip over the drain cover that's still not mended, not even after Mrs Housden's three letters to the council. Last time she's going to walk past the corner shop and wish she had fifty pence for a popsicle.

She turns up her front path, sees the pile of bin bags outside the front door, ready for the charity, pushes open the door and hears Sadie yakkety-yakking to some customer about last night's telly, Minnie hoovering up the hair with a plastic toy and a pretend motor sound in her mouth.

"Will you pack it in?" says Sadie, and the motor stops. Then, "That you, Birdy?"

Birdy braces herself, treads carefully into the kitchen, worried what she's done now, what Sadie's found. Can't be the phone, 'cause that's snug in her pocket, or the charger, 'cause that's in her bag. Could be the box, with the teeth and the clover and the photo of Fitz. Could be that, Birdy thinks. *Don't let it be that, don't let it—*

"You want to start packing," Sadie says, teeth full of hair pins, so the words come out thin and stretched like they've been strangled. "I want you packed this weekend, ready for the van Monday."

"Oh." Birdy breathes in relief. "That."

Sadie rolls her eyes, goes back to pinning Gina Heffernan's hair on the top of her head, like she's swirling cream on top of a knickerbocker glory. Goes back to the telly talk and whether Phil should leave Marlene or stay for the kids.

Birdy turns and scuttles upstairs. Her secret's safe, but still it sends sparks spitting into her, flickers of electricity that buzz–buzz–buzz in her brain, speeding her heart and racing her veins. Because this is it. The last time she'll have to hear Sadie's voice drip with disappointment, feel her eyes on her, wide with disapproval, watch her love Minnie fatly and fully and a hundred times more than she ever cared for her.

She'll miss Minnie, she s'poses. She'll miss Dad, even. She'll miss him telling her tall stories, telling

179

her the tale of Dorothy flying up in her house and then down the yellow brick road to meet the Wizard of Oz; she'll miss him making her cheese on toast and burning the crusts no matter how many times he tries to get to it in time; she'll miss him whispering into her hair and telling her she's special, she's his Birdy and one day she'll fly high as them all.

But those were all before, weren't they, when it were just her and him, and sometimes Grandpa. And she don't have hair now and, besides, he's not even her dad, is he? He's a fake, a fraud, a Great Pretender, like Dorothy's wizard, who turned out to be nowt but a small, old man.

But Fitz? He's still got magic and more. She pulls the photo out the box, checks it again to make sure. Yes, she can feel it in her. He's the one, she knows it. He's her dad and tomorrow he'll take her up in his arms and tell her the story of him and her and why and what and who she really is. Then the future'll be set, all new and shiny, and always the bright side.

She slips the picture into the pocket of her rucksack, then pops the clover in and all. Then a pair of jeans and two T-shirts, some pants and a vest and the slip-slop deodorant that smells of clean, and last the train money: twenty-five pounds from her savings jar, money that were meant for a phone of her own. But she'll not need it, will she, already got one.

Birdy takes stock of it all, and nods, satisfied. Marilyn she'll fetch in the morning, but from now on, this is all she needs. Not that skirt that Sadie got her "just in case she felt like dressing nice" and that's now no more than moth food at the back of the wardrobe, not her school uniform, and not that flaming *Who am I?* booklet, neither. 'Cause she'll have a new story when she starts school again, one that Fitz'll give her.

So this is it. This and the address that's typed out black and white on an email and's now neon-lit in her mind; mapped out and all, just a walk from Waverley station.

"Broughton Street," she mouths to herself.

That's where she's headed, straight up the train tracks and true.

And one way only.

Home.

Chapter Twelve

It's not even six when Birdy sets off, her dad not due back from shift, nor Sadie awake for two hours yet, and if Minnie stirs, she'll just trip-trap down stairs and switch the telly on so she won't be any the wiser, neither. But still Birdy feels sick when she slips out the door in the dark, sicker still when she closes it knowing it's for the last time. But then she snatches at the thought of him – at Fitz – and feels her heart swell with the hope of it all, feels it light up the dim streets like a beacon, and so without looking back once, she steps past the stupid sign, out the gate, and down the road to the loft.

*

She'd hoped upon hope he'd be in the chair when she went to fetch Marilyn, that he'd have heard her godless prayers and come running to say his goodbyes, sing his song, tell her a story one last time.

Dogger, that is.

But all that's to be found is the thrum and hum of thirty birds, awake and watching her with their liquorice-allsort eyes, wondering what she's up to so early. She feels her heart shrink a little, feels the courage begin to seep out, like water from a leaky pail. How's she going to thank him now? How's she going to make sure he's okay? Make sure he knows where to come to visit?

If he'll come to visit.

She waits then, counting down sixty elephant-seconds in the hope he's just tripped over his laces or got his wings caught on a hawthorn. But a minute passes and the air is still slack and there's still nowt but space where a boy should be.

She could falter now, fumble and give up, like her old dad slapping the books shut and putting the kettle on instead. But that's just it, in't it? He's her *old* dad, and what'd be the point of flapping back there with her tail-feathers trailing? No, she's going to do this, even if it is just her and her bird. And with that she scoops Marilyn from her perch and pushes her into the carry-box.

"Goodbye," she whispers to the others. "Be good for Harry, eh? Be fast."

"We will," the birds tell her with their bobs and their curtseys.

"I'm sorry about Billy Bremner," she says. "Tell him for me, will you?" And she thinks of the man asleep in the house behind them. His lungs might be rotting but his heart's strong and full of love and even if he in't her real grandpa, he's the grandest man she's ever met. "I'm sorry for everything," she says. "Tell him that."

But the birds have gone back to their preening

and pecking, back to their bird business, leaving
Birdy to hers.

"Come on, then," she says to Marilyn. "We'd
best be off. 'Fore he wakes, eh?"

Marilyn says nowt but Birdy knows it's a yes,
and so, soft and swift, she slips through the dust
and out the door into the day.

The gate clacks as she closes it and Birdy looks
up at the window, waits for it, but the curtains
don't twitch even a bit and so she hurries on
towards the station, not right, past Manjit's –
'cause she knows he's up, knows he'll be looking
out, trying to catch her, catch up with her, to tell
her not to go – but left, down Wilton Street, and
on into town to the station.

Dad'll have her note by now. *Gone to the loft*, it says
in shaky black biro. *Probably not back 'til tea, 'cause
we want to do an extra toss.* She hopes it's enough,
hopes he can read it, hopes there's nowt Sadie's got
in mind for her that'll send her flapping to the
phone or round the corner trying to grab her back.

'Cause she'll not be there, will she?

She'll be gone.

The station's full, day-trippers milling and picking at food, and up in the high rafters pigeons peering down, as if it's their loft and the people're the imposters. Birdy hoicks her rucksack on her back, hushes Marilyn in her basket, not that she's mithering much, no more than on any other journey, and she's done a few, though nowt long as this.

Birdy clocks the ticket machine – Manjit says a machine's better than a man or a woman, won't ask questions: "Why're you going there?" "Why're you on your own?" "Your mam know what you're up to?" – presses the button for "Destination", types out "E-D-I" and then it's on the screen already, she don't even have to finish the word.

She clicks it, clicks the button for "Child", feeds in her money, gets her three pence or so change. She's checked the departure ten times if she's checked it once, and it's stayed the same for each: 09:27, it leaves, 09:12, it is now. She's fifteen minutes to spare, to get herself to platform four, on to a carriage and into a seat. She don't need food – got Manjit's chews for that, and a biscuit she got from the tin – or water, 'cause she always carries a bottle. Dad – that man – told her that: "You never know when you'll thirst and you'll die quicker of no water than no food." She's checked and it's true: just three days she'd live without water. Though it's only three hours to where she's going, where there'll be a whole fridge of food, and a choice of drinks, not just plain water all the time.

That's when it happens, a lurch in her stomach, like it's maybe thinking about all the food she might have and saying, "No, ta, not just yet." Only it's not food that's making Birdy swirl so, it's the terrible enormity of what she's doing, where she's going. Suddenly the two hundred and twenty miles stretches to more than a million, the three hours to a lifetime.

She's changed her mind, can't do this, after all. A skinny little scaredy-cat, she wants to run back to her grandpa, to her almost-dad, even. He'll do, won't he? It's not like he's an ogre or a villain. Just tired from ferrying people about, ferrying Sadie and Minnie. Even Sadie's not so bad, when you think about it. Not like she's Cruella de Vil, even if she don't like birds, says they're dirty, would rather they were in a feathered cap or, worse, a pie.

She's not going. She can't. She'll ask for her money back, turns to find someone to help, but crashes *smack* into—

Christ on a bike!

"Dogger?"

'Cause it's him, it's really him, stood there like Robin Hood with his hands on his hips and arrows on his back and a cap to cover his stubbled skull.

"Aye," he says, cock of the walk. "Who else would it be?"

"How ...?" Birdy tries to decide which question to ask first. "How'd you find me?"

"I heard you, din't I? Talking to . . . that boy."

"Manjit," she tells him, though she knows he knows.

"Whoever. Anyway, I had to come then," he says. "Not going to let you do something like this on your own. I'm not scared," he adds. "Not like . . . him."

Birdy considers this, the luck of it, the loss she'd assumed. "I thought you'd stopped talking to me."

"No." Dogger shakes his head so the feather in his cap quivers. "My mam were . . . she weren't right. Still not. But I've got a while, I reckon, can see you safe to Edinburgh, to Fitz's door."

"I weren't . . . " Birdy begins. "I . . . "

But she don't finish it. Instead she feels the slip of his hand into hers, his fingers, bone-thin, tighten around her own. "Death or glory," he says.

Birdy feels herself fill to the brim with bravery. "Death or glory."

And like that, hand in hand, hearts fat with

valour, they make their way on to the train, a boy and a girl and a bird.

The carriage is only half-full so they each get a seat, but there's none for Marilyn – she's got to go in the luggage rack up high.

"Be good for her," Dogger says. "What she's used to, up there."

The man opposite, with the big nose and the gold rings, don't look like he thinks it's good for anyone and nor does the mam with the two little 'uns, messy-haired and twittering about trains and toilets and, "Are we nearly there yet?" Birdy ignores them all, gets out her phone and a book – *The Fanciers' Manual* – settles down to read. But the lurch of the train sends her skittering again and she has to look out the window to stop herself feeling sick.

"Look at all them houses," Dogger says. "All them people."

Birdy looks, watches them shrink in the

distance, 'til they're no bigger than ants, so small she could squash 'em.

"Bye, people," Dogger says.

"Bye, houses," Birdy adds.

"Bye, Casey Braithwaite."

"Bye, Sadie."

"Bye, ants."

Birdy looks quick at him, sees in his eyes that he's in her head, right in there. She'd been a fool to doubt it. She smiles then, lets him lift her mouth 'til it's a grin as wide as the waters of Leith, as Portobello Bay in the pictures that Manjit found for her.

"Thanks," she says.

"It's nowt," he replies.

But it isn't nowt. It's everything, and they both know it.

"Can I have a go of that?" Dogger's bored and fidgeting in his seat, needs distracting and's seen her phone, a shiny toy to him.

"Go on, then." She pushes it towards him. "But don't delete owt."

She watches him as he clicks this and that, flipping from app to app, page to page, things she's not even bothered looking at herself.

"Careful," she says.

"I am," he insists, though he's not, throwing the phone from hand to hand.

The mam's looking at them, face frowned down. The big-nosed man and all.

"Put it away," whispers Birdy. And he does then, slips it in his pocket.

But the mam's still staring. "Where're you off to?" she asks.

Birdy rummages in her head for something that'll shut her up. But the truth seems as good as anything, so she tells it. "Edinburgh," she says. "To see my dad."

The mam nods. "He and your ma not together?"

Birdy shakes her head, 'cause it's true, in't it?

"I'm not with their dad, neither. Darryl," the mam says. "It's life, in't it? You have to make do."

Make do, Birdy thinks. That's what Grandpa says: *Make do and mend.* When he's fixing planks or netting, or darning a hole in his sock. She puts him out of her head, can't think about him, not any more. All that's done, behind her. In front's the future.

In front is Fitz.

Birdy's stomach's filled with wings by the time they pull into Waverley station, hundreds of them: birds or butterflies, she don't rightly know, but whichever they are they're fritted, flapping and sending her nerves a skittering.

They don't stop when they get off, don't stop when they find their way through the labyrinth and escape into the thin, watery light of the Scottish sky, don't stop when they see the castle on the hill, glowering down, the crags, black behind.

Birdy shivers and zips up her hoodie. She's a long way from Leeds.

"The people here talk weird," Dogger says, as Birdy traces the map from memory, right along Princes Street and then left to St Andrew Square. "And it smells weird and all. Like cat food."

"It'll be a brewery," Birdy tells him, snatching facts from Manjit's mind, offering them up like a sacrifice that might calm her nerves, still her slightly. "There's one in Leeds, en't you smelled it?"

But he en't.

And it don't calm her nerves, neither. She's a bundle of 'em as they turn down Broughton Street, tread carefully down the wide stone steps to 14a.

"Ready?" Dogger asks.

"Ready as I'll ever be," she says.

She lifts a trembling hand, pushes down on the bell, hears it ding-dong, ding-dong, in the distance.

"He's coming," Dogger says, breath hard and fast as her own. "I can hear him."

And she can too: his footsteps clacking on flagstones, the rattle of a chain.

Then the turn of a handle, the creak as the door opens wider, wider, wider.

And then he's there. Just as she pictured. His hair shorter, mind, and his skin lined, not the smooth of the photo or the picture online. But him, still.

William Fitzsimmons.

"Oh," he says, like she's not what he expected. "Hello."

"We've come . . . " Birdy begins. "I . . . "

But neither of them work, neither say what she wants, get to the point of it all. And the point is . . .

"Hello," she says. "I'm Bridie. And I think you're my dad."

Chapter Thirteen

"I'm sorry. What?"

"I'm Bridie," she says quick, 'cause repeating that's the easy bit. "Bridie Henderson. Well, it were something else but I changed it back. Bonnie, she's my mam. And this here is Dogger. And ... and ... I think you're ... " She's struggling now. Saying it once were hard enough but now summat's got hold of that word and won't let it out. " ... I think you're my—"

"Dad," he says. "I heard. I just wasn't sure I believed you." William Fitzsimmons's face's gone funny and he's running a hand through his curly hair, pushing it back like it's fretting him, though it don't fall any further than the top of his forehead.

"Can we come in, then?"

The man looks up behind Birdy then back at her. "We? Is your mum here?"

Birdy nudges out an elbow to shunt a word out of Dogger but it hits air, shunts nothing.

Dogger's gone.

He said he'd see her to the door but she didn't think he'd meant just that, thought he'd stick around, 'cause he's always thirsting for adventure and this is the greatest of them all. Well, of any she's had, anyway. But now she feels something slip from her, a bone, maybe, or a tendon, something that kept her straight and strong, 'cause now all she is is weak and wobbling and worrying what she's done.

But then she brings another boy to mind, clings to him and his fine words and kindness. She's come this far, en't she? the Manjit-in-her-mind says.

She stares at the man here in front of her – the dad she's been missing – and so she can't mess it up, she's got to get herself inside, got to.

"No," she says, firm as she can. "It's just me." Then she remembers, lifts up the basket. "Well, me and Marilyn."

"Marilyn?" His face is still funny, funnier as he peers at the carry-box, trying to see inside. "Is that a cat?"

"No." Birdy shakes her head. Lifts the lid a peek. "She's a pigeon, see?"

William Fitzsimmons does see. "Oh, well, I don't think she can come in. There's . . . rules. No pets," he adds quick.

"She could go in your garden?" Birdy suggests. "She won't be no bother."

"Garden?" He laughs. "You're standing in it."

"Oh." Birdy looks at her feet, at the five granite steps and the stairwell with its bins and black bags. Not forty foot, not even fourteen.

"You can come in," he says, his face softer now,

199

less strange. "Because clearly we need to talk. But you'll have to leave the bird out here for now."

For now. Birdy clings to those words like they're sticky candyfloss, sweet and spun by magic. "Will she be safe?" Birdy asks.

"From what? Cats?"

"Aye, and thieves."

"Thieves?" Fitz gives her another look. "I don't suppose anyone'd steal a pigeon."

"You'd be surprised," Birdy says. "Harry had two nicked out of his loft – Ant and Dec – reckons they're in France now."

"Oh, well." He nods, like he believes her but don't want to. "I think she'll be safe," he says. He's got his teacher voice on, sort of calm and in charge, and so Birdy does what he says and pops Marilyn on top of a bin. For now. She'll talk to him about a loft later. But first things first.

"Come on, then," he says.

And she does.

*

The flat is long and thin and cold, with grey stone on the floor and white ceilings so high she can barely see 'em, and there's no photos on walls or mantles, just weird shapes of stone – sculptures, she thinks. But she were right about the books, there's plenty of them, stacked neat in shelves along the corridor and some on the floor besides. More books than Birdy can shake a stick at. And it fills her with a gleaming certainty. That he's the one – her dad. Because he reads, and not just fairy stories for four-year-olds but grown-up books, and stacks of them.

"Have you read them all?" she asks.

"What?" He looks to where Birdy's looking. "Oh, yes, I suppose I have. Do you read?"

"Oh, aye," Birdy says. "All the time. When I'm not with the birds, that is. Though sometimes I read to them and all."

"I bet your mum loves that," he says.

Birdy pulls a face. "Sadie?" she says without thinking. "You must be joking. She don't bother

201

with books. And my dad—" She stops herself. Because he's not, is he? Not any more. And Sadie's not . . .

She realises what she's said soon as he does. "Sadie?" he says, his face funny again. "You mean you don't live with Bonnie?"

Birdy feels herself waver and wobble, like she's gossamer blown on the breeze of his words. "Sadie's my stepmum. She's a mobile hairdresser. But Bonnie, she's . . . " She looks at him, her eyes pleading, willing him to know what words she's lined up, like Dogger does, so she don't have to say 'em out loud. But he don't. He's not in her head. Not yet. "She's dead," she finishes.

"What?"

"She's dead," she says again, quieter, as if it'll help the words not to hurt. "She died when I were three."

"I don't . . . " The man sinks down into the sofa, pale face in his hands. But when he looks up he's red and raging, and it's at Birdy. "It was you, then? It was you sent the emails ... Pretending to be her? D'you know that's illegal? Do you know how much trouble you could be in?"

The sentences slap her — *smack-smack-smack* — each one stinging, each one making her eyes smart. "I'm sorry," she pleads. "I'm sorry. I had to ... " She tries to remember what Manjit said, why they were doing it, sees him grinning at the keyboard, hears him explain. "I had to get your attention," she says. "That's it. That's what I were doing. If I'd just said it were me you'd not have written back or even noticed."

"I would have," he says. "Jesus, of course I would have." He hits his fist into the cushion and Birdy can see his eyes are wet. "I need a drink," he says then, standing. "Do you ... do you want something?"

"Have you got water?" Birdy asks. "From a tap in the fridge?"

"Well, yes, but from a normal tap."

"Oh," Birdy says. "You're all right, then."

203

He shakes his head, like she's a mystery to him, which she is, she s'poses. Then he disappears out the room, off to boil the kettle, it turns out, 'cause Birdy can hear it rumble and sing. When he comes back his eyes are dry and he's got a cup of tea, but not brown like Sadie and her dad, green with a paper tag hanging out.

"What's that?" she asks.

"Peppermint," he says. "Do you want some?"

Birdy shakes her head. Toothpaste's bad enough, let alone drinking the stuff.

He takes a sip, sets it down on the table with a clank. "So," he says. "You'd better tell me everything."

"Everything?" There's so much, Birdy thinks, hard to squeeze all of it into her thoughts. Which is odd when you think about it, 'cause she couldn't find two sentences to write in Miss Higgins's booklet. "What shall I start with?" she asks.

"How about you start at the beginning?" He tries a smile, and it's thin and feeble, but it's still a smile. "Go on, sit down." He nods at an armchair, low and leathery.

"All right, then," she says, settling herself into it. She takes a big breath, and shuts her eyes. "Once upon a time . . ."

She tells him all she knows, which adds up to not much, after all. That her mam had her and then she died and then Dad had her, and then Sadie come along and Minnie after. And now there's another on the way so they've to move away to the other side of town, away from Grandpa and his birds. Only she found the birth certificate that says he's not – her dad, that is – so she got to thinking.

"And you thought I might be your dad?"

"Aye." Birdy nods.

"Why?" he asks. "What made you think that?"

"This." She slips the photo out of her rucksack, holds it out.

He takes it from her carefully, grips it like it's precious or porcelain-thin, like it might crumble

205

or disappear – *poof!* – in a puff of nothing. "She kept it, then," he says, voice weak with wonder.

"Aye," Birdy says. "Must've. I found it in the envelope. With the certificate."

"Were there others?" he asks. "There should have been. I took lots."

Birdy shakes her head. "No. I don't think so. Though Sadie come back and I had to pack up quick."

"Hang on," he says and disappears off again, down the corridor and back, *clip-clop*, but bouncing now, a trot, not a trudge or an angry stamp.

"Here," he says, when he bounds back in. "Look."

He hands her an album, red with gold edging.

"What's this?" she asks.

"Open it," he tells her. "Go on."

Heart dancing faster than a cat on a hot tin roof she lets it slip into the crease of her thighs, pulls the pages apart, as if magic and mayhem might fly from them, fill the air with sparkles and spells.

They do.

Because there, smiling back at her, is a woman, the same woman in her photo, only this time she's in fancy dress – a pirate – with a stripy top and gold hoops hanging from her ears and a paper parrot sewn on one shoulder. She remembers now – has seen this photo before in the box with the shells and the glitter when Mam were still alive. There's another of her and all, cross-legged on a lawn, book in her lap – like Birdy's sat now. She can't see the camera in this one, is too busy reading whatever it is, too lost in the story. Each time Birdy flips the pages, there's more of her, and her friends too, a whole gang of them grinning and gurning and fooling for photos. Fitz is in some of them but not as many, 'cause it's his camera, she s'poses, his eyes on Mam. And that's a shame, she thinks, being as it's him she needs to know about now, him that's been missing all this time, the piece of puzzle that will slot in snug to fill that hole.

"Did you . . ." She tries to grasp the word, to hold it down, but it keeps flying away from her. "Did you—"

"Did I love her?" he finishes for her. "Yes, I did. But not the way you think. Or, no. I did love her like that, but she didn't love me back."

Birdy feels it slipping away from her, tries to grab it before it falls through her fingers. "But are you—"

"No," he says, quick. "No, I'm not your dad, Bridie."

Birdy feels a wash of loss through her, wet and cold and stinging, feels the hole gape black and hungry and wider than ever. She closes the album. "So . . . so who is, then?"

William Fitzsimmons sighs. Not a cross sound, but a sorry one. "Your dad worked in a pub in town. Leeds, I mean. He used to be into sport."

"Swimming," Birdy says, with a sigh of her own. "He were a swimmer."

"Yes, that's right. He was a swimmer but he'd

had an accident. I think your mum liked the sorrow in him. She thought she could fix it."

"She didn't," Birdy says. "Fix it, I mean."

"No," he says, like he knows that's not even possible.

The questions bubble up in Birdy. "So why's it not say he's my dad on my birth certificate?"

Fitz shakes his head. "That's something you need to ask him, Bridie. There's a lot you need to ask him by the sounds of it."

"He won't answer," Birdy says. She can feel the tears coming now, too close to the surface so they're starting to spill out. "He never does."

"Bridie," he says.

"It's Birdy," she says then, the truth of it sinking in and stinging.

"Birdy," he repeats. "That fits. Birdy, does anyone know you're here?"

She swallows hard, wipes the snot. "Aye," she says.

"Who?"

209

"Manjit," she mumbles.

"And he's . . . ?"

"He's in my class at school," she admits. "But he's not daft or owt. He's dead good on the internet. He's the one that found you."

"Bridie . . . " He's smiling, only his forehead's creased up, and she knows he's not happy. "What I mean is, do any grown-ups know you're here?"

She shakes her head. "No. Just him and Dogger."

"Dogger?"

"Aye, he were with me when I knocked on your door, but then he run off – home, I reckon."

"And will this Dogger have told your dad, d'you think?"

She shakes her head. More likely to see pigs flying or pigeons with curly tails.

"You know we need to call him, don't you? Your dad."

Birdy nods. She don't like it, but she knows it.

"I can do it," he offers. "Just tell me the number."

"It's on my phone," she says. And she reaches into her bag, rummages, pulls out nothing. "Oh." She stands then, tries her pockets but there's nowt there either, just some empty chew wrappers and the train ticket.

"It's gone," she says, her voice cracking and a sob slipping through. Then she remembers. "Dogger had it, on the train, He were playing with it. He must've kept it."

"Hey, hey, it's all right," says Fitz. "So you'll get it back when you see him. Tell me the number and you can use my phone."

It's not all right, though, is it? 'Cause she don't know the number, has never needed to. "I en't got it," she says. "Not in my pocket and not in my head, not anywhere."

He hands her some toilet roll. "I'll look it up," he says. "What's his name? Tommo?"

"Aye," Birdy says. "Tommo Jones."

"Jones?"

William looks at her like she's having a laugh but there's nowt funny, is there? Birdy nods.

"Do you know how many Joneses there are in Leeds?"

Birdy blows her nose. "A hundred and fifteen," she tells him. "Listed, anyway. Manjit checked," she adds when she can see he's bamboozled. "When he were putting numbers in my phone. But there's only two on Beasley Street and the J Jones is Jerry and he's ninety-seven and deaf so he won't answer even if you do try."

"Well, I'll be . . . They give the house number," says Fitz. "It's all there, look." He holds out his phone.

Fitz makes the call. Goes to the kitchen to "protect her ears", and she's waiting for the shouting and the "sorry"s, even though she don't rightly know what Fitz's got to be sorry for, it weren't his idea, any of it. And she's glad then that Dogger's gone so Dad can't be cross with him and all, 'cause him and

Dogger don't mix, like oil and water. He's never wanted him round and never let her go round Dogger's, neither, not even keen on her meeting him in the loft, though there's nowt he can do as he won't go up there himself to stop it. Even though she tells him Dogger's all that stoppers the hole, all that makes her feel full and right . . .

It's quiet, too quiet – no shouting coming from the kitchen and in here it's just the tick-tock, tick-tock slowness of the clock on the wall.

Fitz comes back in. "No answer," he says.

For a second Birdy feels relieved wings stretch in her, a soar of joy.

But Fitz don't look anything like joyous and she's back down to earth with a tumble and a flap.

"I'll try again in a bit," he says. "You sure you don't know a mobile number?"

Birdy shakes her head.

"And you don't have an answerphone at home?"

"Minnie broke it," she says. "She were using it as a spy transmitter or summat."

Fitz nods. "I suppose we'll just have to wait." But he don't look like he's up for waiting, got a jiggle on him, a twitch.

Then Birdy remembers the bird she's left in a basket, and thinks of something, another way.

"Can I have some water now?" she asks.

"'Course." He reaches up to a cupboard. "Pint glass do you?"

"I'd rather it were in a saucer," she says.

He looks at her as if she's told him the moon's made of cheese.

"It's for Marilyn," she says. "My pigeon?"

"Right," says Fitz. "Right you are." And he fetches her a saucer, walks with it to the front door, careful not to slop a drop, but he won't put his arm in the basket.

"She won't bite," Birdy tells him. "Can't. No teeth, see?"

"It's not the biting I'm worried about. It's the pecking. And the ... disease."

"She's not got disease," Birdy says, bolshie and

bullish. "She's cleaner than you or me. Well, me, anyway. Though I did 'ave a shower two days ago."

Fitz laughs. "Daft, isn't it? A grown man scared of a bird. Still, I'd rather not."

"Here. I'll do it." Birdy takes the saucer and holds it out for Marilyn who drinks, cautious but quick, thirsty, after all.

"So she's your pet?" he asks.

"One of 'em," Birdy says. "Though she's not a pet, mind, she's a racer, a working bird. There's thirty all together, thereabouts." Then she remembers. "'Cept one less, 'cause of Billy Bremner."

"Billy Bremner?" he asks. "Leeds United captain nineteen sixty-six to nineteen seventy-six?"

"Aye? D'you know him?"

"The pigeon, no. The man, yes. I was named after him. My dad was a Leeds fan. Me too. It's why I went to uni there. Why I met your mum at all, I suppose."

215

Birdy goggles at the impossibility of it, the smooth, round perfection.

"You know she was from round here, don't you?" he says then.

"Who was?"

"Your mum."

Birdy looks around her, shakes her head, can't believe this, don't want to, in case it's a joke or a trick.

But he don't say, "Ha ha, I were fooling you!" He just nods. "Glasgow," he says. "Bit different from here and a few miles away. But Scotland, still." He looks down at his shoes, like the truth's in the gleam, raises his head and she can see the sadness, deep in him. "I thought I'd bump into her one day, you know, just walking along the street. But ... "

Fitz looks down, lost in his thoughts of her mam, Birdy reckons, sadness swelling.

"We could fly Marilyn back with a message for Dad," says Birdy. "If you like?"

She thinks he's going to say no, tell her they've to wait inside, silent on the sofa or summat. But instead he stands, brushes his hands on his corduroy trousers and says, "You know what, Birdy Jones?" he says. "I would like that. I would like that very much."

Birdy writes the note: Fitz's address and phone number, and a few more words besides:

Tell Dad I'm sorry.

She holds the bird as Fitz rolls the note like she's showed him, slips it into the ring. Then they let her go, toss her up high on Calton Hill and watch her wheel and turn in the sky as she gets her bearings. At first he's worried she don't know where she is or what she's meant to be doing, but Birdy tells him to be patient, to have faith. So he finds his faith and he waits, and she waits with him, and Marilyn too, perched on the monument

217

pondering it. Then — *abracadabra!* — she's soaring south, and swift with it.

"She's going home," Birdy tells him.

"Just like that?" he asks.

"Aye," she says. "Just like that."

Just like me, she thinks, and with those words her heart sinks, tumbling from the sky like it's shot.

But Fitz sees, and catches it. "Do you like burgers?" he asks.

"Aye?" says Birdy, like it's obvious. Because who don't?

"Me too," he says. "And we've missed lunch, so I reckon we could treat ourselves, don't you?"

Birdy nods, lets him lead her back to Broughton Street, to a café in a basement like his own. Lets him buy her a burger and a milkshake, so thick you can stand your straw in it, can spoon it into your mouth like ice cream.

"Birdy?"

"What?" she asks, the straw still in her mouth.

"I was wondering," he begins. "Shall I tell you some things I know about your mum?"

Birdy lets the straw drop and nods, mouth as wide open as her ears, as she waits for the story – the true one, this time.

"Once upon a time ... " he begins, "There was a beautiful girl called Bonnie."

By the time he's done, Birdy knows ten more facts about her mam; ten gems that gleam like gold in her pocket to add to the three she's been clutching:

1. That she could speak French, but only when she was wearing red lipstick.
2. That she didn't really like dogs or cats; what she really wanted was a marmoset or a monkey.
3. That she could do cartwheels and the splits and often did in corridors on campus.
4. That she didn't eat meat.

219

5. That she did eat liquorice, sometimes so much her teeth were black as soot.

6. That she hated church and football.

7. That she loved the sea and hoped to live near it some day.

8. That when she danced, it was like watching a doll or a dervish, so mesmerising was she.

9. That sometimes she got so sad and angry she'd shut herself in her room and no one would see her for days.

10. But then she'd come back smiling and singing and doing the splits, and they'd call her their Bonnie Princess and watch as she dazzled them all.

"Why'd she get sad?" Birdy asks, as they let the café door clank shut with its cowbell ding behind them.

"I don't know," said Fitz. "She didn't seem to know either."

"I like liquorice," Birdy says then. "But not so much my teeth go black. Though I like aniseed balls more. D'you think she liked them and all?"

"I expect so," says Fitz.

Birdy smiles, satisfied, 'cause she must've got that from her mam, and that's something to hold on to, something real. Though even that don't fix it.

She's still not full, not whole.

She reaches out then – does it without thinking – lets her fingers slip into his, lets them tighten and don't let go, so they're walking, hand in hand, bird basket dangling from the other arm, the few yards back to the flat.

That's when it happens.

"Birdy?" comes the shout.

She stops dead like she's shot or stunned with a ray-gun, so that Fitz pulls out of her hand and she's on her own. Just her and the man stood at the bottom of the steps, with his wide swimmer's shoulders and his Leeds top.

Then he drops his eyes from her, looks instead at Fitz. "What the flaming hell do you think you're doing with my daughter?"

Chapter Fourteen

For a second, Birdy soars as she works out Marilyn must've made it home in less than an hour for him to've got here so speedy. But then her head's back from the clouds and she sees her dad again, sees he's set to smack Fitz – *bish-bash* – right in the face, he's that mad. And he's big – bigger than Fitz, anyway; a good head taller and a few stone heavier and all, so she don't rate Fitz's chances much. But it's not his fault, none of it, so she's got to stop it, and so before anyone can throw a punch or even an insult she's there on the steps, blocking Fitz and facing up to her dad. "Don't," she says. "Don't shout, it's not him, it's me, it were my idea."

"Yours and your friend's, I'm told."

"What?" She's baffled now, 'cause there was nowt about Dogger nor Manjit in that note.

"Oh, aye," her dad says. "Your grandpa were straight round when you didn't turn up for cleaning. Sadie's going spare," he adds, though Birdy's not sure that bit's the truth, but she's not sure her dad lies, not any more.

"So it weren't Marilyn, then?" she asks. "Who told?"

"Marilyn?" he asks, blank-faced. "No, it were Manjit."

"Manjit?" She feels something in her sink. Her bird's not the fastest, and her best friend's not the best, after all.

"Aye, who else?" he says, like she's stupid. "So you've got a phone and all," Dad adds. "But you've not been answering."

"No," she says. "It got . . . lost."

"I think you should come in," Fitz says quick, before Dad can say owt to that. "Have a talk."

"Oh, aye," Dad says. "Don't you worry, I've got a few things to say to you."

"But—"

"It's all right, Birdy," Fitz tells her. "I'll explain."

Birdy's not sure what Fitz is explaining in the kitchen while she's sat worrying on the chair, her hands all sweaty and her stomach a sickly soup of milkshake and meat, but when Dad comes out the beet-red and bluster's been bleached out, so his face is pale as Sadie's slimming milk and stone-set.

"Get your things," he says to her, voice thin as a reed.

Birdy gets 'em – her bag and her basket – goes over to him where he's waiting by the door.

"Sorry for the bother," he says to Fitz, who shrugs and shakes his head.

Birdy feels a nudge at her back then, pushing a "Sorry," out of her, though she keeps her head sunk so she's looking at the scuff of her shoes when she says it, so she can't see them, either of 'em, when they say, "I should think so and all," and tell her all the reasons she's got to apologise.

Though nowt comes but a pat on the shoulder – from Fitz, she clocks, when she turns to him, his long, fine fingers, soap-scrubbed nails resting on her top, sending his own sorry straight into her.

"Cab, now," says her dad, sending Fitz's hand off and her to the door.

She opens it to go then has a look back, swift, so she can see what might've been: at the wide flag floor, the books, the bareness of the walls – a life waiting for her to step into. But she weren't the right girl, after all, to fit it, and he weren't the right dad.

And this one is. She don't rightly know how yet, but he's hers, so Fitz says, and she's to go with him. And she does, straight up the steps to where the cab's waiting, squatting on double yellows, a ticket already slipped under the windscreen wiper, telling them off, telling them they've to pay a fine.

He snatches the ticket, then slams his door, not a word from him as he buckles them both up, starts up the engine.

"I'll pay for it," Birdy offers. "The parking, I mean." Though she don't know how or when.

But he's staying schtum, words stoppered up as they pull away from the pavement and swerve in a semi-circle, back up the hill.

And that's how they stay, both of them, silent and staring ahead as they cross the city, past the black cavalcade of castle and crags, then up through the grim-grey of the suburbs and into the expanse of bracken brown between there and home.

Four hours fourteen minutes it takes them, four hours fourteen minutes of air so thick with what's unsaid you could slice it like butter and serve it on toast. But it's not 'til they've parked up and sat, still buckled in, still staring at nowt, for another three minutes, that a word comes out and it's from Dad and it's this: "Listen," he says.

And so she does. As he tells her about how he and Mam met, all of it, in pin-sharp glittering detail. Tells her about the times they had together, and apart, because he was a mess after his injury, and no one could help him, not even Mam. Tells her about the sadness when Mam died, the great hollow hole he felt open up inside him, and only Birdy could fill it.

Birdy knows what that's like. Sees he's like her, after all. So she takes a breath, and a leap with it. "So you are my dad, then?"

"Aye," he repeats. "Of course I am."

She can't see him then, 'cause her eyes are still fixed on Mrs Venables's fence, but she can hear that he's crying, can feel it, even, the tang of tears in the air, like salt on a sea breeze.

"So why're you not on the certificate?" she demands.

"The what?"

"The birth certificate. I saw it in the envelope. It said 'Unknown' so what were I supposed to think?"

"Oh, Birdy." He lets out a sob that catches in her throat too, makes a lump when she tries to swallow. "I don't know. We weren't together, see, not by the time you come along. Not because I didn't love your mam, you need to know that. But because ..." He pauses, scrabbling for the right words, for any words " ... because I was a great lummox, too wrapped up feeling sorry for myself over the swimming. And I should've changed it, when your mam went, and I got you, but it were enough to learn how to make fish fingers and beans without burning them; how to do you a bath. And your mam had put it in her will, for me to have you, and no one else ever asked. Besides, I knew you were mine so that were all that mattered."

"I s'pose," she says, though she don't at all.

"Could you not see it?" he says. "Weren't it obvious?"

Birdy looks at him as if he's the mad one now. "But we're nowt alike," she says. "Minnie, she's like you, and like Sadie. But me, I'm no one's, am I?"

"Oh, Birdy, you are!" He puts his hand on her leg and she flinches but don't shove it off. "You're mine. You're mine, d'you hear? And I'm sorry if that's ... a disappointment. Sorry if you'd rather Mr Fitzsimmons or ... someone else, but I'm your dad and nowt's going to change that."

Birdy's shoulders start to shake as the first wave of it washes over her.

"Come here," he says then, unbuckling them both. And he pulls her tight to him, so he can squeeze the crying so hard it gives up, though it takes a while and she's sniffing still when she sits back on her side.

"Dogger," she begins without thinking. "He reckoned you – my real dad – were King of China."

Dad's quiet then and she claps an invisible hand

over her gob, tells herself she's an eejit for saying it – saying his name. But this time he don't shout at her, don't tell to stop the Dogger nonsense and stay away. This time he opens her door, tells her to come with him, and Birdy's more scared of saying no than where he's taking her, so she does as she's told.

She guessed they were going to Sadie, that she were going to tell her off for running away and tell all the reasons why Dogger were bad news, and why it were his fault she'd gone bad and done this terrible deed, but they don't stop at the front door, nor the back one, neither. Instead they're straight to the shed and the stacks of boxes that never got unpacked when they moved in the first place.

Dad tells her to wait on the grass, and she does, counting the seconds in her head 'til he comes out the shed again, a box in his hands.

A shoebox.

So covered in seashells and glitter you can't see the cardboard.

Birdy feels her world swerve, tip slightly, as if it's spinning off course.

"It were your mam's," her dad says, sitting down next to her, not knowing she knows it already. "I didn't keep it in the house, 'cause I were afraid of what were in it. Daft now, it seems."

Birdy shakes her head; it's not daft, 'cause she's still scared, and she can tell by the tremble that he is and all. "Don't you know, then?" she asks.

"Aye," he says. "I know. I looked in it all the time when you first come to live with me. Couldn't stop myself. But Sadie said I were making it worse by the dwelling, told me to put it away 'til I were fit enough and you were old enough. Only that day came and went and now look where we are."

Birdy looks, sees them sat on the lawn in a house that's not their own for much longer, their eyes red from crying and ringed with tired, sees the daftness of it all.

"And it's not Sadie's fault," he says. "None of

232

this is, you've got to understand that. It were all me, trying to protect myself. And you and all."

"From what?" Birdy asks.

"This," he says, and lifts the lid on a life that were hers, once, and is about to come flooding back.

The first pictures she's already seen, 'cause they're the ones Fitz showed her, then there's more – Mam as a girl, no more than Birdy's age, she s'poses, but her hair proper long and twined in braids.

"Who's that?" Birdy asks of the woman next to her.

"That's your mam's mam," says Dad. "Died long before you were born, so I never met her."

"And she lived in Scotland?" Birdy puts two and two together.

"Aye," says Dad. "But your mam never went back, not after that, and not once she'd got you. Said it gave her the willies."

Birdy laughs, 'cause he's said that word, but the laugh gets cut off short and turned to a choke when she sees what's next, what Dad's got in his hand, holding it like it might catch fire or turn into a serpent.

It's a photo, of baby Birdy this time, sat at Mam's feet, and she's wearing a paper crown and a skirt so orange you could squeeze it for juice. 'Least Birdy s'poses it's her but it's hard to tell, 'cause next to her, holding himself up on Mam's leg, there's another one – another child.

But this one's got shorts on. And wellington boots. And on his back, a pair of wings.

"Who's that?" she asks, pointing, her finger touching the gloss as if she can feel him, can work it out for herself.

But she can't, can't fathom it, this other baby – this boy – and what he's doing in her picture, in her life.

Her dad takes a breath, takes Birdy's hand, which sends her nerves scattering and her heart pitter-pattering, ready to run. "That," he says, "is your brother."

"Brother?" The word flick-flacks from her mouth, bounds around in front of her, just out of reach.

"Your twin brother," he tells her again. "Dougie."

Dougie, she says in her head.

Dougie, she repeats.

Dougie, Dougie, Dougie, Dougie. Dogger.

Dogger.

And it's so clear and sharp it cuts her – *slash* – straight across the chest.

"Oh," she says. "Oh . . . Oh."

"It's okay," her dad tells her. "I know it's hard, but you have to understand. Do you? Do you understand?"

Birdy shakes her head, 'cause she knows the kernel of it, the truth-seed, but the rest of it all is just fluff and blur and she can't quite grasp it, see it for what it is.

"Dogger don't live near the loft," says Dad. "He lives in here." He touches her head. "And in here." Then her chest.

Birdy sees a vision of a boy then, his halo of blond hair glinting with red, lit up like an angel by the summer sun, sea water splashing so fierce she can feel it slosh against her own pudgy, puppy-fat thighs. "But ... " begins Birdy. "I don't ... I don't—"

"He died, Birdy, when you were both two. A car accident."

"Were I there?" she asks, breathless with loss and want.

Dad nods, squeezes her hand. "Aye," he says. "But there were nowt you could've done, nor your mam. So don't go thinking there is."

Birdy's thoughts are a dozen a minute but that weren't one of them. "Is that why she gave me to you?" Birdy asks. "'Cause she didn't love me as much as him?"

Dad laughs, half-sob, half-snot. "No, no, Birdy. She gave me to you 'cause she *did* love you. She loved you more than you love birds."

Birdy knows how much that is, more, maybe,

than she loves Dad, and she feels a prick of needle-sharp guilt at that.

"But she were ill," Dad carries on, "and knew she didn't have long and she said I'd do a better job than anyone could, though I told her I doubted it."

Birdy's quiet then, thinking of all them years that've passed, all the things that her dad's done and the ones he hasn't.

"You've not done too bad," she says finally.

"You think?"

"Aye," she says. "I do."

When they go back into the house at last it's dark enough to see the stars, and Birdy's so tired Dad has to lift her over the doorstep, set her in a chair, where he leaves her and the shoebox while he has a word with Sadie, tells her what's what.

When Sadie comes in, she's sorry and all, gives Birdy a wordless hug and a kiss on the top of her stubble that makes her lips tickle and she says so and laughs.

"You give us a scare," she says as she tucks Birdy into bed as if she's no bigger 'an Minnie.

"I know," Birdy says. "I didn't mean to."

"I know," says Sadie, an echo that's as warm as the wind in August.

Her dad comes in then to say good night, like he did once upon a time, full of the job of being a dad, of checking she's got water, that she's not got nightmares before she even starts dreaming.

"I'm okay," she tells him, and means it.

"I believe it," says her dad. "'Cause you know what you are?"

Birdy shakes her head so her brain bangs the walls of it.

"You're audacious," he says. "The audacious Birdy Jones."

Birdy sucks in sharp at that, remembering it, hears it slip from Miss Higgins's lips. But she never thought she'd hear owt so fancy from her dad.

"Where'd you get that word from?" she asks.

"Yer mam," he says. "That's what she called you and Dogger. The Audacious Twins."

"What's it mean?"

"Look it up," he says. "But in the morning, mind."

Birdy sighs. "All right," she says, rolling on her side ready to sleep. Then she remembers summat else. Summat Dogger told her. And Fitz and all.

"Did Mam sing Bob Marley?" she asks.

"Aye," her dad says. "Why?"

"Sing it," she says. "Will you?"

"Blimey, Birdy, not sure I've got the voice."

"Please?" she asks, and this time he don't argue, just closes his eyes to find the words and the notes from a time long gone, and then, when he opens them, his mouth opens and all, and he starts to sing.

And as soon as he does, Birds feels the tears bubble up and burst out of her, because it's the one she thought, the one about the three little birds, and it's not because she's sad or because she scared, because she's not now. It's because she knows the words are true.

'Cause she might have lost her mam, and a real dad that never was, and a friend who never even existed.

But what she's got is a family, one she's going to be part of from now on, Dad tells her, official-like, with a new birth certificate with his name on and adoption papers so's Sadie can be her proper mam, if she wants. And if she'll help him fill 'em in?

And she's got summat else and all.

A brother.

And together, they fill that chasm so it closes up for good and she is whole and knowable.

And because of that, every little thing is going to be all right.

Chapter Sixteen

She don't get a chance to look up "audacious" when she wakes, 'cause Grandpa wants to see her. He's left a message with Sadie on the telephone so she knows it's serious, 'cause he don't use that 'cept for bird business or when he had to call 999 for Mr Menzies next door when he fell down the stairs.

Dad's coming with her, don't want to let her out of his sight 'case she runs again, though she's promised not to, but he's promised Sadie and so that's the end of it. So it's both of 'em trotting round the corner to see what's what and why the old man's so mithered.

"There you are," Grandpa says when they step into the thick, sweet fug of feathers and seed. "Got summat to show you."

"You won't believe it," Manjit tells her, his voice shy, 'cause he knows he's probably in the doghouse with her and with her dad and all.

But she gives him a grin to tell him not to mind, not now.

"Is it Marilyn?" she asks. "She got back, didn't she? How fast did she do?"

"Aye, she's back," says Grandpa. "And she did nicely. But that's not what's got us dancing. Here."

He beckons Birdy over to the far pens, where the fledglings nest and where old birds or sick birds are kept in quarantine, resting up away from the flap and the faff of the other birds.

Birdy peers in, Dad behind her, his hands on her shoulders, Manjit behind that, hopping with it he's so happy.

"You see?"

Birdy looks. And then sucks in a gasp because she does see.

And what she sees is Billy Bremner. Thin now, fragile, and some of his feathers gone, but him all the same.

"He came back!" she says.

Grandpa nods. "Told you he would," he says. "Only go one way, do pigeons."

"Aye," she says.

"And what way's that?" he asks.

Birdy smiles. "Home," she tells him. "They only fly home."

Death or Glory

She watches her dad tack down the netting, his forehead frowning with concentration, his fat hands deft, after all; careful with the hammer and nails as he is handling the birds. Instinctive, Grandpa reckons, always was, just like Birdy. Sadie does a massive shudder when he says that, tells him she hopes he's not passed it on to the baby – Joe, he's called, after Grandpa, which is the bees knees, Birdy reckons – 'cause more birdbrains is the last thing they need. But she's smiling when she says it so Birdy knows she don't mind, not deep down, long as the feathers don't come in the kitchen.

And, besides, Joe's bound to love the birds, she knows it, 'cause he's her brother. And brothers? Well, they just do.

They've nearly done – just the flypen to go – and in a week the birds'll be brought over in Grandpa's van. 'Cept the three Manjit's bagsied for his own flock. His mam and dad weren't too keen at first but Grandpa said he could keep them round his as long as he liked, long as it were him that cleaned them, and he'd give him a ride up Cop Hill for tosses. So Billy Bremner's staying put, and Grace Jones, his lady. Fitz and all, who's flying now, and fast with it. But Birdy's not mithered, 'cause she'll see 'em when she goes round Grandpa's for tea, or Manjit's, 'cause she's always welcome there, he says. He don't even mind about the phone, reckons it weren't worth much, anyway, so his number's in the new one she's got for big school, and she messages him, and Fitz and all, when she's got a question Dad can't answer.

"Right," he says then, wiping September sweat

off on his T-shirt. "That's enough for today. En't you got a booklet to finish?"

"Aye." Birdy sighs, though it's not turned out too bad, after all. Full now, it is, packed with family: Mam and Dad and Sadie and the young 'uns – Minnie, and now Joe. Grandpa and the birds too. The birds take up five pages, truth be told, what with all the facts she's put about them. So many, Miss Higgins got her to read it out in class and bring Marilyn in so they could all meet her, and even Casey Braithwaite wanted to touch her belly, soft as a pocket, hear the coo of her, the comfort.

Dogger's in there too, with a photo of them both sat fatly on their mam's lap. She remembers now, 'least that's what she tells herself, remembers she couldn't say his name right, nor him hers, so Dougie turned to Dogger and Bridie to Birdy and they somehow stuck. She knows the Dogger from the loft weren't real either, just an imaginary thing, formed from fragments of memory and clothed in hope. That's what the doctor told her and Dad, anyway, and said it was quite normal, given everything. Though he don't come to visit no more, not even at the loft, and Birdy's sad about that. But Dad's right, he weren't the best influence with his swearing and his swagger, and, besides, she's got Manjit now, by her side in school and out, full of facts and bubble gum and bustling to be with her and the birds all he can. And there's Minnie and all, who never did owt wrong in the first place except be good at swimming, and who's helping Birdy learn now, just like Birdy helps her read.

And now there's Joe, whose eyes might be all Sadie's but there's something of Dogger about him in the way he smiles.

She's only got one bit to go. The words to describe herself. Her and Dad come up with a list but they all agreed there was only one word that stood out, bright and glowing and shouting to the world just who she was.

Audacious, she writes, and then, dog-eared dictionary open, copies out its synonyms.

"What's a synonym?" her dad had asked.

"Words that mean the same thing," she'd said. "Like they're related."

"Like you and Dogger."

"Aye," she says. "Kind of. Or me and Minnie or Joe ... or me and you."

Dad smiles at that, goes off to get tea, lets her get on.

And so she writes, sounding the words out to herself as she goes, satisfied with who she's turned out to be:

"Plucky," she says. "Intrepid."

"Bold and brave."

"Daring."

"Fearless, unflinching, intrepid and wild."

"Valiant."

And then, at the last, she stops, her breath stuck, her pen dropping a clot of ink that spreads wide, then smudges.

She has to check twice to make sure she's read right.

But it's there in black and white, and now in looping blue on in her booklet:

Death or glory, it says.

"Death or glory," she echoes, a whisper to Dogger who she knows listens, even if he don't show.

Then Birdy lets the ink dry, closes the book.

Who am I? asks the cover.

Birdy smiles. "Me?" she asks back, then answers herself, clear as a catcall. "I'm Birdy."

She puffs out her chest, proud as a pigeon, and full to the brim.

"I'm the audacious Birdy Jones."

Acknowledgements

With thanks to Catherine Bruton, Liz Kessler, Helen Stringfellow, Sarah Geraghty, Ruth Pelling, Wendy O'Shea Meddour, Nic Watkins, Jude Savill, Jo Holbek, Rachel Davis, Boo Lightfoot, Dandy Smith, Anna Wilson, Elen Caldecott, Julia Green, Karen Ball, Samantha Swinnerton, Sarah Molloy, Julia Churchill and all the other incredible hens who have helped Birdy and me to fly, and find a home.